"FREDDIE O'NEAL IS ⟨ P9-DFU-456
McGEE." —award-winning author David ...

"YOU'LL LIKE FREDDIE. She flies. She drives a motor-cycle. She takes no flak from anybody."
—BARBARA D'AMATO,
author of the *Cat Marsala* series

"A UNIQUE, ENGAGING CRIME SOLVER . . .
TERRIFIC." —bestselling author Judith Kelman

## Don't miss the other Freddie O'Neal Mysteries by Catherine Dain . . .

### LAY IT ON THE LINE
*Nominated for a Shamus Award by the Private Eye Writers of America*

"APPEALING CHARACTERS AND AN INTRIGUING PLOT . . . A WINNER." —Linda Grant

### SING A SONG OF DEATH
"A FAST-PACED STORY with touches of wry humor and poignancy . . . wonderful characters . . . what more can a reader ask for?" —Maxine O'Callaghan

### WALK A CROOKED MILE
"A superbly written P.I. novel." —Carolyn G. Hart

### LAMENT FOR A DEAD COWBOY
"Catherine Dain has done it again, only better. I am capti-vated." —Margaret Maron

### BET AGAINST THE HOUSE
"Read *Bet Against the House* and it's no gamble. You'll win." —Michael Connelly

# MORE MYSTERIES FROM THE
# BERKLEY PUBLISHING GROUP . . .

**CAT CALIBAN MYSTERIES:** She was married for thirty-eight years. Raised three kids. Compared to that, tracking down killers is easy . . .

*by D. B. Borton*

ONE FOR THE MONEY
THREE IS A CROWD

TWO POINTS FOR MURDER
FOUR ELEMENTS OF MURDER

**ELENA JARVIS MYSTERIES:** There are some pretty bizarre crimes deep in the heart of Texas—and a pretty gutsy police detective who rounds up the unusual suspects . . .

*by Nancy Herndon*

ACID BATH

WIDOW'S WATCH

**FREDDIE O'NEAL, P.I., MYSTERIES:** You can bet that this appealing Reno private investigator will get her man . . . "A winner." —Linda Grant

*by Catherine Dain*

LAY IT ON THE LINE
WALK A CROOKED MILE
BET AGAINST THE HOUSE

SING A SONG OF DEATH
LAMENT FOR A DEAD COWBOY
THE LUCK OF THE DRAW

**BENNI HARPER MYSTERIES:** Meet Benni Harper—a quilter and folk-art expert with an eye for murderous designs . . .

*by Earlene Fowler*

FOOL'S PUZZLE

IRISH CHAIN

# The Luck of the Draw

# CATHERINE DAIN

**BERKLEY PRIME CRIME, NEW YORK**

THE LUCK OF THE DRAW

A Berkley Prime Crime Book / published by arrangement with the author

PRINTING HISTORY
Berkley Prime Crime edition / March 1996

The Putnam Berkley World Wide Web site address is
http://www.berkley.com

ISBN: 0-425-15230-8

Berkley Prime Crime Books are published by
The Berkley Publishing Group,
200 Madison Avenue, New York, NY 10016.
The name BERKLEY PRIME CRIME and the BERKLEY PRIME CRIME
design are trademarks belonging to Berkley Publishing Corporation.

PRINTED IN THE UNITED STATES OF AMERICA

10 9 8 7 6 5 4 3 2 1

## AUTHOR'S NOTE

While there is a University of Nevada campus in Reno, I have fictionalized it in all respects—except for some minor geographical ones—for the purposes of this story and other stories in the Freddie O'Neal series. Any resemblance of persons or events depicted herein to actual persons or actual events is purely coincidental.

# Chapter 1

"CURTIS, I JUST don't understand what it is that you do. Why would a television station hire a business school professor as a consultant when you don't know anything about television?"

"Because I know something about people, about organizations, and the way they interact," he said patiently.

One of the things I really admired about Curtis was his patience with questions, although he didn't see it as patience. He saw it as genuinely liking to come up with answers—the mark of a born academic.

"Have you decided?" asked a cheery young waitress with a long black ponytail. She was wearing a short green dress with white ruffled sleeves and a white ruffled bodice. Someone's idea of the well-dressed colleen.

"Not yet," I said. I wasn't ready to break the conversation. Once she had nodded and walked away, I added, "And what do these people expect you to *do* about their interaction?"

"Have you ever watched the Channel 12 evening news?"

1

Answering a question with a question was another sign of an academic mind.

"Sometimes. The woman with the frosted hair and the guy who looks like a ski bum in a suit."

"The woman with the frosted hair is Brianne McKinley, a highly popular, highly paid anchorwoman. She's a bigger star than Lane Josten. The ski bum, as you called him."

"And he doesn't like that?"

"Well, he doesn't seem to mind. He doesn't seem overly ambitious, and he certainly makes more than minimum wage."

"Then what's the problem?"

Curtis waited for me to realize that the problem was that I kept interrupting before he could finish. When I did, he continued.

"Brianne doesn't get along with Steven Burns, the newly hired program director, something no one bothered to find out before throwing them together in tight quarters. Both of them have contracts, and the station doesn't want to buy either one of them out. More than that—Steven Burns's contract doesn't say so, but everyone agrees, including Horton—that Steve was led to believe he'll be the next general manager of the station when Horton Robb, the current station manager, retires." Curtis paused for dramatic effect. "I've been hired to intervene. They want me to come up with a way that McKinley and Burns can interact professionally, without their mutual antipathy affecting the job performance of either one."

"You mean you have to convince two kids who hate each other that they have to share their toys?"

"Something like that." He smiled, although I don't think he really liked the analogy.

"Good luck."

"Well, failing that, worst case, management wants me to negotiate an amiable parting of the ways with Burns." He picked up his menu, a large sheet of laminated parchment bordered with shamrocks, and put his reading glasses on. "Aren't you hungry?"

"They don't want Burns to sue when they break his contract." I toyed with my menu, not sure what to order. Curtis had warned me the restaurant served mostly fish, and I had agreed to try it. If I could try dating, I could try a restaurant that didn't serve beef. I wondered what the connection was supposed to be between fish and the vaguely Irish theme.

"You are fond of cutting to the heart of things, aren't you?"

"I'm sorry. It's my automatic response to circumlocution, or what even sounds remotely like it. Do you mind?"

"No, no, of course not. In fact, I find it challenging. Challenging in a good way, I mean."

We would have stumbled around several more exchanges, each wanting to make sure we hadn't screwed up the datespeak idiom, but the waitress returned.

"Need more time?" she asked.

"What would you suggest for somebody who isn't really into restaurant fish?" I responded.

"The salmon and the swordfish are both fresh."

"Flown in today after sitting how long in a boat?"

"How about the bay scallops with fettucine primavera? The sauce is light, the scallops were individually quick frozen, and if you don't like the scallops, you can push them to one side." She wasn't the least bit offended by my comments.

"You got it," I said.

"House dressing on your salad?"

"Sure."

While Curtis ordered a poached salmon filet—he evidently didn't share my vision of fish turning cloudy-eyed in the middle of the hold—and chose a wine, I looked around the restaurant. Or what little I could see of it. The wooden walls of the booth were high, shutting off the booths on either side, and the ones across the aisle were staggered in a way that made it hard to see both occupants at the same time. The light on the table had a fluted orange shade, barely enough to read by. Soft sounds from the piano in the bar filtered in through hidden speakers. A date restaurant. I was actually in a serious date restaurant.

A thought crossed my mind, that there was a proper way to behave here. It had died by the time the waitress left.

"But what do you *do*? When you walk into the station tomorrow morning, what happens?" I persisted.

"If I'm any good, nothing. I watch, and they do just what they would do on any other Monday morning."

"How long do you watch?"

"As long as I need to. Once they're used to my presence, I ask questions. I ask Brianne how she sees the problem with Steve, ask Steve how he sees the problem with Brianne, ask Lane and other coworkers for their observations."

"Here we are," the waitress said, presenting the wine bottle for Curtis to inspect.

He put his glasses back on to make certain the label was what he wanted, then nodded. She deftly twisted the cork out and handed it to him. He sniffed it and nodded again. She splashed a little in his glass. He swirled it and sipped.

"That's fine," he said, smiling at her.

She poured me half a glass, splashed a bit more into his, stuck the rest of the bottle in an ice bucket, and left. She smiled back at Curtis before she walked away, and I felt a twinge of jealousy. I didn't want to feel it, but I was jealous of how easy the ritual was for her.

I tried the wine.

"You could have ordered beer," Curtis said.

"No, really. I'm getting a kick out of drinking this stuff. What is it?"

"Chardonnay. The word is becoming almost synonymous with American white table wine, but this one has some character."

I stared at the glass. "Personality, too."

"Well—yes, I suppose you could say that. There is something arbitrary about the words used to describe wines."

"Like 'acquired taste'?"

"I'll find the waitress. You really want a beer."

"No, I really want to figure out what people see in wine."

He looked at me thoughtfully. "I don't suppose it would help if I talked about primal echoes of Dionysian revelries."

"I'll keep trying." I raised my glass. He clinked his against it. The wine still tasted like cold, thin, fruity acid as far as I was concerned. "Now. Back to the TV station. You said you were going to watch for a while. Then what?"

"I can't answer that. I don't know what I'll find."

"Really? Do you make it up as you go along?"

"Close enough," he sighed. "I'll give you a progress report in a few days."

That stopped me—the words "in a few days," and how casually he said them. Curtis Breckinridge and I were in some sense of the phrase "seeing each other," and I was clearly having more trouble with the sense of a university professor—especially one who taught something as shapeless as leadership studies and couldn't even explain what consulting was about—dating a private investigator than he was.

Maybe I just had more trouble with dating than he did.

"What's happened with the neurotic?" he asked, just as the waitress slipped salad plates in front of us.

She blinked, but walked away with professional grace.

"Nothing, so far. I was finishing something else, and I haven't started on the case. All I know is that she quit her job and moved. And she didn't leave a forwarding address with the post office."

The neurotic Curtis was asking about had been a psychologist's patient who skipped on a bill for several thousand dollars. The shrink had turned the account over to a collection agency, which had hired me to find her.

"And what are you going to *do*?" He smiled again, to let me know that he hadn't really felt needled by my questions. He kept smiling as he ate his salad, which was a pretty neat trick.

I liked to watch him smile. Curtis had such an open face, round cheeks and brown eyes with friendly crinkles, and the smile seemed to run all the way up to his receding hairline. Watching him smile made me feel good.

"Make it up as I go along. You're right. That works as well as anything. But I'll probably start with something simple and shopworn, like asking her neighbors if she gave anyone a clue as to where she might go."

"Doesn't the psychologist have a clue?"

"I'll talk with her, too. She didn't offer any help to the collection agency, but she might come up with something if asked directly. The problem is confidentiality—I'm not sure how much information a psychologist can give without breaking the law."

"Probably not much. That puts her in a serious bind, if she really wants to collect. Why did she let this person run up such a big bill?"

"Well, I guess I can ask her that, too."

We smiled our way through the salads and into the main course. I realized as I tried to get the first bite off my plate that the scallops hadn't been a great choice. The fettucine had been led past the boiling water by a chef who took the words *al dente* seriously. I couldn't get it to twirl on my fork. And I couldn't cut and scoop, either. The pasta was as stiff as the julienned red and yellow peppers, which had also been led past the boiling water on the way to the plate. The scallops were okay, and the sauce was as light as promised.

I might have complained if I had been alone. As it was, I took small bites, chewed well, and smiled.

I was doing my best here. Curtis Breckinridge was a nice man, and so many things in my life had crumbled when I tried to grab hold of them. I didn't want seeing Curtis to be one more. In late-night arguments with myself, I pointed out that by being less assertive and disagreeable than I might normally be, I was setting myself—and Curtis—up for a possibly unpleasant surprise. The answer I offered was that if I just eased into it, we might both get used to the water before it got too hot—or too cold.

Or whatever it turned out to be.

I sat there as quietly as possible, not squirming, when he paid the bill. After a couple of serious discussions on economics and obligation, we had agreed that since he earned approximately twice what I did, he would pay for two out of three evenings. I didn't really like sitting while he paid—I didn't really like waiting for him to pick me up when it was his turn to drive, either—but I was trying to accommodate, as best I could.

Sometimes I walked to wherever we were having dinner, and then let him drive me home.

Not that we were having dinner all that often. Maybe once or twice a week. And not every week. We had met in June, and Curtis had been out of town a lot during the summer, doing research for a book. Now that he was settling in, waiting for the semester to start, we were having dinner a little more frequently. Just often enough that my friend Deke Adams had noticed I wasn't around the Mother Lode coffee shop as much as I used to be.

Just often enough that both Curtis and I knew we were going to have to take action pretty soon, one way or the other.

I suspect—or would like to believe—that things are easier in cultures where people either have sex right away, casually, or don't have sex until some ritual takes place. Cultures where there are definite, agreed-on guidelines. But two people in Reno, Nevada, in the late-twentieth century, out of their teens, with some ambivalence about commitment, have to (one more time) make it up as they go along. And we were both doing our best.

I kissed Curtis goodnight in the car. We had started kissing goodnight a couple of weeks earlier, but nothing passionate had followed, and we were even a little stiff about kissing goodnight. If I'd let him come to the door, I would have had to kiss him goodnight all over again, so I just told him that I wanted to get an early start on the case and opened the car door.

"I'll call you tomorrow," he said.

"Sure," I answered. "Talk to you then."

Butch and Sundance were waiting on the porch rail, glaring at the car. Curtis had tried to make friends with them, but cats sometimes get perverse when people do a "here, kitty" number. Mine had so far refused to share the house with Curtis. If he came in, they went out.

Anyway, Curtis hadn't been inside enough times for Butch and Sundance to be a problem.

They raced ahead of me through the office that took

the place of a living room and jostled each other down the hall toward the kitchen.

I opened cat food for them and a beer for me. The wine had left me wanting a drink. I took the bottle into the bedroom and turned on the television, flipping channels to find something that would lull me to sleep. Catching sight of bright yellow letters advertising *The Maltese Falcon*, I thought for a moment that something was wrong with the set. I paused long enough to see a picture postcard shot of the Golden Gate Bridge, followed by a closeup of a ruddy Humphrey Bogart with a cigarette dangling. I flicked away. I hoped somebody would stop Ted Turner before he got hold of *Schindler's List*.

The least objectionable movie was an old horror flick. I watched until a scientist with a handy gun in his lab shot his wife dispassionately, straight through the heart, because he suspected a monster had taken control of her. That was enough. In fact, it was almost enough to make me join NOW. I gave up and turned off the light.

I got a restless night's sleep, but I was ready to go to work in the morning.

The psychologist—Helen Stern—had a soothing message on her answering machine, promising that no one else would hear whatever words were left on the tape, and that she would check often and get back to me. I told her who I was and where I was headed and promised to call again soon.

The neurotic, as Curtis had dubbed her, was one Darla Hayden. Her last known address was an apartment on Artemisia Way, just west of the university. The building was a concrete and brick two-story, with no landscaping, and a "Vacancy—One Bedroom" sign out front. It had probably been constructed with the latest university expansion in mind, maybe even right on top of the crumbling apartments that housed the last generation of students.

I had a vision of archaeologists excavating the site as if it were Troy, discovering layers of student detritus dating back for a century, from CDs on top through tapes and LPs to the old 78 rpm records, then an old gramophone horn, shreds of sheet music, and a single piano key on the bottom. Textbooks written before computers, before Neil Armstrong set foot on the moon, would be buried in the lower foundations of an old sorority house, next to the hair curlers and the half-empty bottles of makeup, still moist with preservatives.

Darla Hayden had lived on the second story. I climbed the stairs and pushed the door buzzer. No answer. The drapes had been pulled back from the window that faced front. No furniture in the living room. The vacant one bedroom that the sign had promised.

I walked back down to apartment 102 and pressed a buzzer above a small card that read "Manager."

"Yes?"

A woman's voice came through the door. I suspected that I was being scrutinized by an eye pressed to a tiny, fisheye opening.

"I'm here about the vacancy." I stepped back so that she could see me.

The door was opened by a short, fat woman in her fifties, with dyed-black hair skinned back from a face that belonged to a bulldog, except for the red lipstick, which had run into the wrinkles around her lips, and the black mascara, which had flaked onto her cheeks. A white dress with tiny blue flowers, the kind that fills long racks in discount stores, hung from her small shoulders but stretched tightly across her round abdomen.

"I just put up the sign. Finished cleaning it this morning. You a student?"

"No. Not for years."

"Well, you never can tell. You look like a graduate student, like the girl that just left."

"I've thought about graduate school. Haven't gotten around to it, not yet."

The woman nodded in approval. "Graduate students make good tenants. They're more mature. They pay the rent, most of them anyway, and they don't have loud parties."

"The young woman who moved out was a good tenant?"

"For almost two years." She leaned closer, blinking her protruding eyes to let me know that she was going to tell me something important. "Everything changed this summer, after she flunked the test—the test she had to take to get her degree. She started being late with the rent, and this month she hadn't paid it at all. I told her she had to pay or move, and one night she all of a sudden moved."

"Just like that?"

"Just like that." She pursed her lips in disbelief. "Didn't even say good-bye, after two years. You want to see the apartment?"

"Yes, thank you."

She picked up a heavy ring of keys that must have been on a table next to the door.

"My name's Dottie, honey. What's yours?"

"Freddie O'Neal."

Dottie nodded, as if the name was acceptable. She led the way back up the stairs to the apartment and unlocked the door.

"A mess. That girl left such a mess, and I never would have thought it of her. She was so nice, all the time studying for her classes."

The living room was spotless. The jungle green shag rug was fluffed, the lime-green drapes glistened with sunlight.

"You've done a great job cleaning, then. What kind of mess?"

"Papers all over. Garbage in the kitchen, moldy cartons from takeout and frozen, she didn't cook. Mildew in the bathtub. You name it." Dottie rolled her eyes up at me.

I shook my head in what I hoped was appropriate disbelief that anyone could treat her so badly. I checked the kitchen, bedroom, and bathroom to make sure that Dottie had cleaned them all with the same vigor. The irreconcilable greens of countertops and linoleum sparkled.

"What do you think?" she asked when I returned to the living room.

"I'd like to take a look at the garbage," I said. When that didn't register, I added, "I'm a private investigator. I've been hired to find Darla Hayden."

"Oh, dear Lord. Is she in trouble? Or are you from the same collection agency that called me?"

I couldn't tell from the tone what answer Dottie wanted.

"I don't know if she's in trouble. Can you tell me anything that might help her?"

"Not a thing, honey, not a thing. She was always so quiet, never had anybody over."

"What about the papers she left?"

"Garbage truck picked everything up a few hours ago, just got it out in time. If I'd known, I'd have kept them for you." She blinked again, leaving more flakes of mascara on her cheeks.

"Is it possible she told one of the other tenants where she was going?"

"I asked, and they all said no. Because of the rent she owed. And the collection agency call." Dottie added that hastily, as if she didn't want me to think she might be a snoop.

"What about friends at the university? Do you know what program she was in?"

"Something about business, that's all I can tell you."

I pulled a card out of my pocket and handed it to her. "If you think of something that might help, give me a call."

"I sure will. I hope she's not in trouble?" Dottie asked again, in the same ambivalent tone.

I patted her shoulder. "When I find her, I'll let you know."

"You be careful, honey," Dottie called as I headed back to my car.

The university business school was small enough— not more than a handful of graduate students—that

Curtis would have to know who Darla Hayden was working with, even if she wasn't in his area. Curtis was spending the day at the television station, so the university would have to wait. Anyway, I wanted to talk with Helen Stern before I pursued the case further.

I decided not to try calling again. I drove to her office. The address was on Court Street, a renovated two-story, Victorian frame house surrounded by gnarled old elm trees that shaded the house from the late summer heat. A card on the front door read: "I am with a client. Please come in and wait quietly. I'll be with you as soon as I can."

The heavy wooden door was unlocked, although a tinkling bell announced my entry. A small foyer had been created just inside, with two more doors. One, closed, said Office. The other was open, displaying a library of sorts, a room with bookshelves along one wall, with an old easy chair covered in faded mustard fabric and a round table beside it the only furniture. Helen Stern had evidently decided that no one steals books.

I picked one at random and sat down to wait. The book was about the women in Freud's life, and the jacket copy promised to explain why Freud didn't understand them. I had barely started the introduction when the office door opened, and I heard Helen Stern bidding good-bye to her patient.

She stepped into the room, a sturdy woman with gray hair frizzed around a sad face. The dark half-moons under her eyes were the only color on her otherwise sallow skin. Her blue cotton blouse and turquoise striped pants looked as if she had put them on without noticing.

"Come—" she started and stopped. "You aren't my client."

"No." I stood and held out my hand. She shook it reluctantly. "I'm Freddie O'Neal, a private investigator. You turned an account over to a collection agency, and there was enough money involved to make it worthwhile for them to hire me."

"Oh, dear," she sighed. "You're the woman who left the message on my machine this morning. I may have made a mistake. Please come into my office, although I only have a minute. I really am expecting a client."

I followed her across the foyer into the other small room that had been carved out of what had once been a large parlor. There was a battered wood desk and three chairs. Not even a couch. Thin white curtains let in the light from a bay window.

She took the chair behind the desk, and I sat in one of the two facing it. The chair wasn't particularly comfortable, not what I would have expected from a shrink.

I waited for her to say something.

"Darla Hayden," she said, leaning forward with a half-smile, as if she hoped I'd help her out. I nodded and waited. "She terminated therapy abruptly, incidently owing me a great deal of money. Her phone was disconnected. I thought a collection agency might be able to find her."

"Incidently? That sounds as though you don't care about the money."

"Well, I do, but I'll be surprised if I see much of it. She just doesn't have it to pay."

"Then why do you want to find her?"

Helen Stern leaned back and shut her eyes. The lids were so blue they might have been bruised. "Because I'm worried about her."

"If you're seriously worried—afraid she might hurt herself—you could go to the police. That wouldn't be a breach of confidentiality."

"I don't want to go to the police. I don't want her treated like a criminal."

"Like a criminal? If she's suicidal, they might send her to a psychiatric hospital, but I don't think they'd treat her like a criminal."

"You don't understand." Helen Stern opened her eyes. "I'm not afraid she will hurt herself. Darla Hayden isn't suicidal. I'm afraid she may commit a murder."

# Chapter 2

SOMEDAY I'M GOING to figure out the line between the personal and the professional. At least as far as issues of trust, loyalty, and ethics are concerned. I know there are people who argue for a double standard—that the Golden Rule may be good enough for relationships with friends, but all bets are off when the relationships are with colleagues or clients. Survival of the fittest—or at least the shrewdest—if not the nastiest. I have trouble with that, and I'd guess a lot of other self-employed people do as well. Friends and relatives can become clients, and clients can become friends. Everybody is a stranger at the beginning, and it's impossible to predict whom you're going to care about.

At some point during the therapeutic relationship, Helen Stern had begun to care about Darla Hayden. That was clear. Her professional obligation—to her client and to the state that licensed her—was less clear.

And I wished she had sorted them out before talking to me.

"Is our conversation covered by any kind of confidentiality rule?" she asked.

"Technically, no, because you aren't my client. The collection agency is. But even if you were, I'm required to report homicidal threats to the police, or at least to warn the person who might be in danger." I didn't remind her that the same requirement applied to her.

"Well, I've botched this, haven't I?"

I let that slide right past.

Helen Stern stared at a spot on the wall somewhere beyond my head. I had the feeling she knew that spot well, that it was the alternative to looking a client in the eye. I had a similar spot on my own office wall, a framed replica of an old Union Pacific poster. I could recite the Platte Valley route by heart.

"Suppose I withdraw the account from the collection agency and hire you?" she asked.

"I don't see how it would help. I'd still have to report the threat."

"Only if you believed she might act on it. And you might have to find her first, to decide for yourself."

"Good thought," I admitted. "But you'd have to pay my going rate of forty dollars an hour, and that would put you further in the hole. I don't know how many hours I'd have to put in on this. Do you really want to add to the debt?"

Helen Stern concentrated on the wall.

"How about barter?" she finally asked. "I normally charge one hundred dollars an hour, but I would do this on a two for one basis. Any two hours you devote to finding Darla Hayden are worth one hour of therapy."

"I can't begin to sort out the conflicts of interest in that," I snapped. "And besides, who says I need therapy?"

"I don't know you, Ms. O'Neal, and I'm not suggesting there is anything wrong that would cause you to need therapy." She lowered her eyes to look at me. "But even healthy people—I could even say especially healthy people—can sometimes benefit from discussing their life situations with a professional. A relationship with a mate, perhaps, or a parent."

"Absolutely not. Somebody pays me to find Darla Hayden, and I don't care whether you pay or the collection agency does, or I move on to something else."

"I'm sorry. I didn't mean to upset you. And this certainly isn't your problem. I have no right to ask you to take it on."

I met her gaze, feeling slightly embarrassed about the outburst.

"If you want to tell me a little about it, I could consider you a potential client. And that would make the conversation privileged."

"Thank you." Helen Stern closed her eyes and exhaled. "I appreciate the decision."

I hoped I wouldn't regret it.

"Would you like tea? A soft drink?"

The front bell tinkled, announcing the arrival of the expected client.

"Would you rather talk later?" I countered.

"No. I'll tell her it's an emergency. I'll just be a few minutes, and I don't have a problem running late with her. I don't have another appointment until three."

"Then I'll take a Coke."

"Is pink lemonade all right? That's what's left."

"Sure."

I listened as Helen Stern explained to someone who didn't seem to mind that she would have to wait. The soft drink took so long that I was starting to wish I hadn't asked. I turned to check the wall behind me. Helen Stern's spot was a Picasso print of two hands holding a few sketchy flowers.

Finally she returned, handed me a sweating bottle of something too pink to be as natural as the label claimed, and resumed both her chair and her story.

"Darla Hayden first came to me four years ago, shortly after she began studying for her doctorate in international finance." She closed her eyes again, and I resisted an urge to take notes. "Getting a Ph.D. is stressful under the best of circumstances, but the pressures are compounded when a woman is invading what is still very much a male-dominated field. I'm sure you can understand that."

She was sure enough that she didn't open her eyes to check my reaction. I didn't volunteer a confirmation.

"Darla made her own situation worse by becoming emotionally involved with the professor who is the local expert in her area, a man with some reputation in the field. He, shall we say, took advantage of her feelings. When it became clear that they could no longer work together, she found herself without a champion in the department. She stayed for another year of course work—a hellish year—because she was determined to finish. Without a champion, however, she couldn't make it through her comprehensive examinations. The department chair informed her three months ago that she would not be permitted to continue."

"I don't understand why she needed a champion to pass comps. I thought people passed them every day."

"And you're right, of course. Most graduate students probably don't need a champion in order to finish a program. But many do, for a variety of reasons. In Darla's case, there were several." Helen Stern opened her eyes to emphasize the points. "She was only the second woman accepted for a doctorate in international finance. The first dropped out because she married a fellow student who was offered a job at the University of Chicago, and she decided to go with him and complete her work there."

"That makes sense. A degree from Chicago would mean more."

Helen Stern smiled, but it didn't make me feel good.

"Yes. But it left the local group saying that they tried a woman, and she didn't work out. They were reluctant to try again with Darla."

"Come on. One woman left for legitimate reasons and they use that as an argument against another? I didn't know anyone thought that way anymore."

"Then you're naive." Helen Stern snapped at me as if she were my mother. I tried not to bristle. "Darla's test scores and credentials—and her own force of character—convinced them to admit her. But when she had an affair with a senior professor, and the affair ended badly for her, she felt the department turned against her. Grading students is subjective at any level, but assessment becomes totally dependent on the judgment of the assessor at the doctoral level. Darla did her best. No one at the university was willing to see it that way."

"Are you sure that her best was good enough? Maybe she just couldn't cut it."

"Ms. O'Neal, do you ever feel that you have to work harder than the men in your profession in order to get the same recognition?"

She emphasized the Ms., as if it had something to do with respect. I took a drink of the pink lemonade, both to break her gaze and to think about my answer.

"Yes. Occasionally," I replied, once I was ready to deal with her. "I also believe that I can do it. And if I couldn't, I'd get out."

"But do you think it's right?"

"I don't think about it in those terms. I think it's the way life is. So I just do it."

"Then I think you're a hero, Ms. O'Neal." She said it softly, leaning forward, elbows on her desk. "You're a hero because you have broken through boundaries that lesser women find impermeable. Darla Hayden wasn't a hero. She could do the work her male colleagues did, she could even go the extra mile it took to get admitted to the program, but when faced with opprobrium over her relationship with the professor who was supposed to be her mentor, she couldn't make that last leap, the one that forces everyone to accept her, break the paradigm, admit the outsider to the club. So you succeeded, and she failed. I admire your character."

I couldn't figure out why, if I were such a success, she

was making me feel so bad about it. More than that, though, I didn't want to talk about me.

"So she wants to murder the professor she slept with?"

"Actually, no." Helen Stern leaned back in her chair, and this time her smile showed a hint of amusement. "She has transferred her hostility to the department chair, the man who acted as her committee chair that last year, although they barely saw one another. Still, he was the person who told her she was out of the program."

"Okay," I sighed. "Give me their names. The professor she slept with and the department chair she threatened."

"The professor is Aaron Hiller, the department chair Randolph Thurman."

"Aaron Hiller? The guy who's quoted on television all the time about our relationship with Japan?"

"The same."

"Okay," I said again. I wanted to think about that before I commented. "The collection agency told me Darla had been working change at the Mother Lode, and that one night she didn't show up for work. They haven't heard from her since. Does that sound like her?"

"Well, it doesn't sound responsible, if that's what you're asking, and under normal circumstances I would consider Darla Hayden responsible. At the same time, she always regarded the job as temporary, she had no attachment to it, and casinos are never in a bind if one person suddenly walks out. That happens so often it isn't even a crisis."

Helen Stern was right about that. Permanent employees at casinos are the exception, not the rule.

"What about friends? Relatives? Do you know of anyone she might have contacted?"

"She has a married sister who lives in Sacramento, but I only know her first name—Sharon. Her husband's name is Joe. She's a stockbroker, he works for the state government in some minor capacity. As far as friends are concerned—" Helen Stern stopped and shook her head.

"Anything else that might help?"

She was silent for a long time.

"I don't know. I'll have to call you."

I gave her my card.

"If I get any information on Darla Hayden, I have to turn it over to the collection agency, you know that. And if there's a serious murder threat, it goes to the police."

"I understand. But I don't think there's a law against giving it to me as well, is there?" She picked up the card and slipped it in her desk drawer. "Or at least making sure she knows that I'm concerned."

"I'll see what I can do."

"Thank you."

We both stood, and this time she held out her hand first.

She walked me to the front door, shielding the entrance to the waiting room automatically, protecting the privacy of her next client.

I was going to have to think about how to handle this.

I drove Court Street to Virginia, doglegged to Wheeler, turned left on High, and pulled into the driveway. I could ask Deke Adams to check the Mother Lode for me, just in case Darla Hayden had confided in someone at work.

But the place to concentrate on was the university. If Darla Hayden wasn't seriously contemplating the murder of her department chair, I could tell Helen Stern that and forget the whole thing. Otherwise, I had to warn Thurman that he was in danger.

Butch materialized as I reached the porch and brushed past me into the house.

My office looked pretty good. A few papers that needed filing were stacked on the desk, and there were signs of gray and orange cat fur on the carpet, but I could tell that my effort to keep things straight was making a difference.

Although I may have tried a little too hard. I had overwatered the new philodendron, and the bottom quarter inch of the paper stack had bonded to the desk. The desk was so battered that the water stain didn't make much difference. I hoped the papers were replaceable.

I left a message for Curtis, on both office and home phones.

He called back about an hour later.

"The person I'm looking for is connected with the university," I told him. "I could really use your help on this."

"Really?"

I wasn't ready for how pleased he sounded. Or how surprised.

"Well, yeah. You know more about the internal workings of the business school then I do."

"I hope so," he sighed. "Although I've only been there a year. Besides, it's always easier to describe someone else's environment than to truly perceive one's own. Or almost always."

"Tough day at the TV station?"

"I'll tell you about it when I see you."

And so I ended up having dinner with Curtis Breck-inridge two nights in a row.

Since it was a Monday night working dinner, I insisted on a fast meal at Harrah's. On me. And I could decide later whether it was expensable.

Not that there was much to decide about. I was back to a hamburger and a beer, and Curtis cheerfully ordered the same, to show me he could be accommodating, too. By the time he arrived, I was on my second Keno ticket.

I had walked over early, and slowly, conscious of my own environment, how much dingier than usual Mill Street seemed in the last rays of the autumn sun. I turned the corner at the post office and headed north on Virginia, giving myself time to choose what it was fair to tell him.

That would depend partly on how much he already knew.

The air-conditioned red haze of the casino sucked me into its timeless chaos by the time I had reached the escalator to the coffee shop. Curtis was right. It's hard to see an environment when you live in it.

I was nursing my first beer as I watched him move between the crowded white plastic tables, looking for me. He was wearing jeans and a blue work shirt, but somehow he didn't look like a Nevadan. I'd have to think about the difference. He walked with the easy lope of a weekend tennis player, long arms hanging loosely at his sides.

When he spotted me, his face lit up.

I waited for him to get settled before I switched to business.

"The person I've been hired to find was a doctoral student last year," I said when the beers—his first, my second—arrived. "Her name is Darla Hayden. Familiar?"

"Vaguely." He frowned, trying to remember. "Tell me more."

"She was studying with Aaron Hiller."

"Oh, God." The frown got worse, rippling all the way from his nose to the crown of his head. "That Darla Hayden. I think the to-do has dissipated by now, but my guess is that no one is going to want to answer questions about it. Are you sure you want to find her?"

"I'm sure the collection agency wants me to find her. And she does owe them money."

"To a psychologist, you said, if I remember correctly."

"Yes." I immediately regretted having offered that information. At the time, it seemed like casual dinner table conversation. I didn't think I'd be telling him her name and asking him for help. One more ethical dilemma. "Does that matter?"

"Well—let's just say it makes sense. I can imagine that a therapist would allow her to run up a bill rather than turn her loose. Wanting to collect is a little puzzling."

I didn't help him out.

"Aaron slept with her," he said, when he realized I was waiting for the story. "Since she was his student, that would have been a mistake, even if she had been emotionally stable. Under the circumstances, it was a nightmare."

"For whom?"

"For everyone, I think. Certainly for Aaron and for the international finance group. And for the student, too. Of course."

"Of course." I didn't underline it, but he flushed. "What makes you describe her as emotionally unstable?"

"A stable person would have accepted the end of the affair quietly and found another professor to work with."

"Why are you so sure a stable person would put her career first?"

He flushed again, a deeper shade of rose. We both waited while the Keno numbers came up. I hit three, just enough to win the dollar to replay the ticket. I pushed it to the edge of the table so the runner could pick it up.

"International finance doesn't often attract people for whom relationships are more important than numbers," he said. "I don't think anyone—least of all Aaron Hiller—expected her to be so devastated when she realized that he would never accept her as an equal. She claims he led her to believe that he loved her. He claims she should have known it was a casual affair, and that she misinterpreted his admiration for her work."

"How do you know what she claims?"

"She circulated a series of memos, in an attempt to muster public support that was truly counterproductive. They were the topic of coffee break conversations for a month or more. I may be able to find some of them for you, although I didn't keep a file. Aaron ignored them publicly, but his answers were circulated privately."

"He really sounds like an asshole."

"Perhaps. A brilliant and well-positioned asshole, however." Curtis tried to keep a straight face, but I almost choked on my beer. I grabbed a napkin, turning as red as he had been a moment earlier. The shared chuckle broke the tension that had started to build.

"So what you meant by calling her emotionally unstable was only that she went public with something that the Establishment had hoped would remain private."

"Essentially, yes."

"I hope you two work this out," the waitress said cheerfully, as she deposited the two plates with hamburgers and fries in front of us.

"What?"

The way she looked from one of us to the other, I think we both asked the question.

"The conversation is so intense," she said. One more person blushing in the southeast corner of the Harrah's coffee shop. The beginning of a trend. "That's all."

I picked up the ketchup bottle and decorated the top bun and the fries.

"What can you tell me about Randolph Thurman?"

"Not what you would call a brave man. He wanted the whole situation to go away." Curtis spread a thin film of mustard on his burger and covered it with slices of lettuce and tomato.

"Does that mean he wanted Hayden to flunk out?"

"Probably. But if you're really asking whether he conspired to flunk her, I can't answer that." He took a bite out of the hamburger. A larger bite than Curtis normally takes. Another answer would have to wait.

"But if Aaron Hiller admired her work, who had the clout to overrule him and flunk her?" I asked anyway, and took a large bite of my own.

"Well"—he swallowed, washing it down with beer—"if Aaron had been there, I'd say no one. But Aaron didn't attend her orals. In her memos, she claims she was the victim of an intellectual gang rape."

"That sounds like enough to make anyone unstable."

"She may have been dramatizing the situation. I'll try to find copies of the memos, so you can judge for yourself."

"Thanks. I really appreciate it, that you want to help."

"I really appreciate it that you asked."

The smile was too much for me to handle.

"So what happened at the television station?"

"I'm not sure." He put his partly eaten burger down and used his fork to cut a French fry in half. "There are so many people running around that it's going to take me a while to sort them out. About all I know at this point is that Steve Burns likes to give orders and doesn't like to say thank you. And Brianne McKinley likes to make decisions without outside input. What puzzles me most is how someone could have thrown them together before settling the ground rules."

"Ground rules? It's a game?"

"Only metaphorically, of course. In a game, the rules would have been set. And some people argue that life is more serious."

That was worth another smile.

"I enjoy talking about work with you," he added.

"Me, too."

"But at some point—and this might be a good time—I'd like to talk about us."

"Us?" I suddenly felt a little queasy.

"Yes." A frown rippled the smile away. "I didn't mean to make you uncomfortable. You must know I care about you."

"I'm not sure what you mean."

"Freddie, I think I understand that you're wary of getting involved, although you haven't said much about prior relationships. And I'm willing to take this slowly, see where it leads. But I want to make it clear that I hope it leads somewhere." His eyes were clear and serious, his round chin unusually firm.

"I don't know, Curtis. I don't know. I like you, but I don't know." That sounded so dumb I wished I could take it back. "Did you have a first step in mind?"

At least I got the smile again.

"I thought it might be time to do something more than a private dinner, sometimes but not always including a movie. The dean is hosting a cocktail party at the faculty center Friday night, a kind of welcome for the new members. Would you like to come with me?"

"It may be complicated—I'm going to be up there this week, asking questions. Are you sure you want me to come?"

"I understand what your job is. And I want you to come."

"Then I'll give it a shot."

His smile got wider, and I stopped feeling queasy. I dipped a French fry in ketchup and ate it.

"Great," he said. "Just great."

I hoped he was right.

# Chapter

# 3

I DIDN'T GO back to the campus until Thursday, because I wanted to catch both Thurman and Hiller on one trip, and I didn't want to alarm anyone unnecessarily. Helen Stern and I would both have had a lot to answer for if Thurman had been murdered on Tuesday or Wednesday, but he wasn't.

In the meantime, I wrapped up a case for a private investigator on my computer network who had been tracking down someone headed for Reno, had dinner with Deke Adams, and watched the Channel 12 news.

Brianne McKinley not only had frosted hair, she had frosted lips and frosted eyelids that barely covered eyes popping with enthusiasm for every story on the teleprompter. Whether it was mayhem and murder, gangs in the public schools, or a cat reunited with its owner, Brianne wanted me—me, personally, I was almost certain—to know about it. That strange projected intimacy had to be her appeal. And her buddy, Lane Josten, didn't have it. When he smiled at the camera, I would have bet he saw his own reflection smiling back.

The rest of the telecast was sports, weather, and segments from a couple of field reporters. I'd have to ask Curtis where they fit in.

When I had dinner with Deke in the Mother Lode coffee shop on Tuesday, I told him about Darla Hayden and asked him to check her out for me, to find out if anyone remembered talking with her before she quit showing up for work. I met him again on Wednesday to get his report.

I walked to the Mother Lode after the Channel 12 News at Six and played three Keno games before he slid his eggplant-shaped body onto the seat next to me at the counter.

"Hardly anybody remembers that girl at all," he said.

Diane, our regular waitress, filled his coffee cup and nodded. If he wanted anything other than a steak for dinner, that was the moment to tell her. He nodded back, and she walked away.

"One more beer," I called after her.

Diane nodded without bothering to turn around.

"How long did Darla Hayden work here?" I asked.

"Three years. Without ever so much as sharing a coffee break. I hear she always had some book with her, and whenever she sat down, she opened it and started reading." Deke slurped half the coffee in his cup and put it back.

"Anybody notice what she was reading?"

"Different books, but often as not they had equations in them. Mathematical stuff. Like she may have been doing some kind of graduate study at the university."

"She was getting a Ph.D. in international finance," I said.

"Ah. No doubt your friend from the university can give you some help, then."

"You mean Curtis?" I knew that was the wrong response, but it came out anyway.

"Curtis. That's the name. Must be getting old. Seems harder and harder to come up with the names of people I haven't met." Deke regarded me through small, red-rimmed eyes that barely made it over puffy cheekbones the color of burnt coffee.

"I'm sorry. Really. One of these days—soon—we could maybe all have dinner or something. But there just hasn't been any reason . . ." I was feeling worse with every word. "I didn't know you wanted to meet him," I finished lamely.

"Not at all, especially if there's no reason." His eyes narrowed into a glare.

New numbers were coming up on the Keno board. I turned away to check my ticket. When only two that I'd chosen showed, I pulled a fresh sheet out of the stand on the counter, marked eight different numbers, placed a dollar on top, and held it up for the Keno runner. Time to start again.

Some people always play the same numbers, figuring they will all come up sooner or later. I always mark at random, and I never look back to see if an old ticket would have won. If you stick with the same numbers, they're going to show just as you're strolling in one night, before you've had a chance to bet. And you can't win without putting your money down.

"I have dinner with Curtis occasionally, Deke, and I like to talk with him." I kept my eye out for the runner. "There isn't anything more than that going on. If you want to meet him, we'll get together. How's that?"

"Fine, if that's what you want to do. You have dinner with him, you have dinner with me, don't seem to be no problem in putting us together."

I knew he was still glaring, but I didn't look back to see.

I waited until the Keno runner had taken my new bet and Diane had put our plates in front of us before returning to Darla Hayden.

"Did you get anything out of Personnel?"

"Nobody there knows nothing except her last check is still sitting in the files. Mailed out and bounced back."

"That's good news for the collection agency. They can attach it. Not so good for actually finding her, though."

"You sound more interested in the girl than the money." A quarter of his steak went into his mouth.

"Well—I would like to find her. I'm going to be talking to a couple of people at the university tomorrow. I'll let you know what happens."

Deke seemed mollified, and we finished dinner in peace.

I thought about stopping to rent a movie on the way home, but I kept walking. I was sorry when I couldn't find anything to watch on television but a movie in which Van Heflin played an old rancher who had trouble figuring out that the peaceful son was good and the son who shot people was bad. I stayed to the end, when

Heflin shot his bad son and cried in his good son's arms. A real tribute to family values.

Heflin didn't get his act together until after midnight, and I almost overslept. I reached the university barely in time for my appointment with Randolph Thurman.

There were two secretaries in the department office, sitting behind desks that trumpeted what a lie the promise that computers would do away with paper had been. The two desks, each with a proliferation of forms and folders, made me feel better about what mine had looked like at its worst.

When I gave my name, the secretary with long dark hair and dangling earrings smiled cheerfully and pointed to an open door.

"He's expecting you," she said.

Randolph Thurman's office was more cluttered than his secretary's. Unlike the desks of some other professors I had known, the detritus consisted more of papers than books. Still, I had never seen a neat office on campus. I wondered if one existed.

Thurman himself was neat, though. His gray hair was slicked back, and he wore a light jacket over his white shirt and pale tie, despite the failure of the air-conditioning to keep up with the September heat.

His bony wrists betrayed the shirt under the jacket as short-sleeved. A minor concession.

Pale eyes were magnified by wire-rimmed glasses, topping a triangular face that reminded me of a tabloid illustration of an extraterrestrial.

I introduced myself, and he gestured toward one of the solid wood armchairs on my side of the desk.

"I've been hired to find Darla Hayden," I told him. "I hoped you might be willing to help me."

"I might be willing to help you if I had any idea where she might have gone, and if I were certain that helping you wouldn't make the university vulnerable to a lawsuit for disclosing private records." His voice was as colorless as his appearance. He barely hit the word "and."

"I'm not asking to see her grades or anything else that could be considered confidential." I paused, hoping he'd blink. He didn't. "I've already been told that she flunked the comprehensive exams for her doctorate. Shortly after, she moved out of her apartment and stopped showing up for work. Have you heard from her?"

It took him a moment to respond, as if the question had to bounce off a satellite first. "Not exactly. I found a potted plant on my doorstep, about a month ago. The note said, 'Peace between us. Darla.'"

"Do you know if she delivered it personally?"

His chin quivered in what I deciphered as a shake of his head. "No one was home at the time."

"Anything else?"

"I'm not sure if I should mention this, but I received a strange message by E-mail."

"What do you mean by 'strange'?"

"Indeterminate. The message appeared about a week ago. 'Are you safe from destruction?'"

"Just that one line? Did Darla Hayden send it?"

"I don't know. Whoever sent it logged on to an account that was set up for a group of graduate students to use on a seminar project last semester. The account had a single password. Darla Hayden was one of the students. I haven't checked with the others, but as far as I know, none of them had a reason to send it."

"Is there some reason you believe that Darla Hayden might threaten you?" I persisted.

That one had to bounce off a satellite, too.

"Since you already know that she flunked her comprehensive examinations, you probably know also that she refused to accept personal responsibility for the failure. She blamed me." His poker face didn't crack. "Because she had exhibited symptoms of instability in other interactions, it occurred to me that the message might have come from her."

"Have you closed the account?"

"No. And I've left the password active. It occurred to me that if it was Darla Hayden, and if she is truly disturbed, she might take it as a hostile act on my part. This way, the line of communication is open, if she chooses to say something more."

"Then you don't really feel threatened. You don't think she might try to hurt you." I probably shouldn't have gone that far. I was right on the edge of betraying Helen Stern's confidence.

Thurman waited for the satellite again.

"I hope she wouldn't try to hurt me," he said.

"Have you thought about going to the police?"

"I considered it. I would rather not. Police and universities can be an incendiary combination. You may find this hard to believe, Miss O'Neal, but I was a student once, and I was witness to a situation that got out of hand when the police were called in."

"Okay. Since you remember being a student, and I

guess that means you also remember how much students depend on professors, I have one more question. Do you really think that Darla Hayden bears the sole responsibility for flunking her comps?" I had argued one side of this to Helen Stern, and I was taking the other side with Randolph Thurman. I wasn't sure there was a right side or a right answer.

The smile was gone. "You're asking me to take a terribly difficult stand. I believe that Darla Hayden took the examination without being properly prepared, and the professors she worked with should look to their own consciences in that regard. I also believe she should have realized that she needed more time and better preparation. I advised her, as her committee chair as well as her department chair, to postpone taking the exam. She chose to take it. She should accept the responsibility for flunking it."

"I see your point. But that's still a pretty tough position, Professor Thurman."

"I'm afraid it's the best I have to offer." He stood and held out his hand. "I hope you find her. And if I come across anything that will help, I'll let you know. I would far rather deal with you than the police."

"Thank you." I stood and shook the offered hand. "Before I go, would you be willing to tell me what you meant when you said she exhibited instability?"

"I'm sorry. The possible lawsuit, you know." His mouth twitched again, almost a smile. He retrieved his hand and waited for me to leave.

"I'll see you soon," I said.

I didn't tell him it was going to be at the dean's reception the next evening.

The cheerful secretary directed me to Aaron Hiller's office, down the hall and to the right.

The door was barely ajar. I knocked.

"Come in!" a deep voice called.

I had somehow expected Aaron Hiller to be smaller— the result of seeing him on television, I suppose. People always look smaller on television, as you watch the dancing image at the foot of your bed. I once saw Hulk Hogan at the airport, when he came to Reno for a wrestling exhibition. I was stunned at how massive he was. Aaron Hiller wasn't in the same class with Hulk Hogan, but he had shoulders a full magnitude broader and more muscular than anything I would have imagined from his appearance on television.

In fact, compared with Randolph Thurman, he might have been Hulk Hogan.

Like Thurman, he was wearing a short-sleeved white shirt and a tie. Unlike Thurman, he had taken his jacket off, exposing his hairy forearms. On television, Aaron Hiller had always reminded me of a Hollywood version of an Old Testament prophet, with his full gray hair flowing into a neatly trimmed beard, his aquiline nose, and his piercing dark eyes.

Standing in front of him, I realized that television hadn't done him justice. The camera had caught only a fraction of his presence.

I could understand why Darla Hayden—whoever she was—had fallen for him. He looked like a heartbreak waiting to happen. And I felt terribly, terribly sorry for her.

Again, I introduced myself, explained my presence in his office, and sat in a hard wooden chair across from a desk. The desk was almost orderly, with papers in low stacks that looked manageable. Two walls of the office were taken up by floor-to-ceiling bookcases, one wall backed a computer workstation, but the fourth wall was the jawdropper.

Most professors have framed diplomas on a wall, and some have a photograph or two as well. But Aaron Hiller had an entire wall of framed diplomas, certificates, letters, and pictures. I didn't recognize any of the signatures or the faces, but they were all wearing suits and smiling.

He waited until I was through looking at his wall before he spoke.

"I'm afraid I can't help you, Miss O'Neal." He smiled as if assuring me there was nothing personal in his refusal. The smile reminded me of Brianne McKinley. "I'm the last person in the world Darla Hayden would get in touch with."

"Why is that, Professor Hiller?"

"We haven't spoken since she fired me as her committee chair and asked Randy to take over. That was well over a year ago." The smile didn't waver.

"Randy is Professor Thurman?"

"Yes. He's the one you should talk to, not me."

"I did speak with him. I wanted to see you, too, because the word is that you knew her rather well, so I thought you'd have some idea where she might have gone."

The smile didn't waver, but the cheeks above his beard turned a pale pink.

"I was involved with Darla's work, not with her life."

"How could you have an affair with her and not be involved with her life?"

The cheeks turned red, and the smile froze. His dark eyes narrowed, and one hand involuntarily clenched. Moses reaching for his rod, to strike the Golden Calf. Except this was Aaron, and Aaron was the one who created the false idol.

"I made a mistake. I admit that. Darla Hayden was a bright, attractive woman. She admired me, she flattered me, and I am embarrassed to confess that she seduced me. I was susceptible, and I have paid for it. My marriage was almost destroyed because of her—because of a minor fling with her—and I am truly sorry it happened." He worked to relax the jaw and the fist. "But I tell you again, I was never involved with Darla's personal life. You can find out more from public records than you can from me."

I was starting to hate the son of a bitch. When a professor has an affair with a graduate student, who then flunks out of the program, a confession of susceptibility doesn't quite cover it. Not when the party line is a demand that the student take full responsibility for the disaster.

"Is there anything else?" he asked.

"Not right now. Would you mind if I get back to you after I've asked around a little more?"

"Not at all. I only wish I could be more useful." He was lying through his smile, I was sure of it. "Darla is so bright—flunking out must have been very difficult for her. I'm certain she didn't handle it well. I hope nothing has happened to her."

"Yeah. Me, too."

Actually, Helen Stern had convinced me that Darla's anger was directed outward, and it hadn't occurred to me that something might have happened to her until he suggested it.

I stood and held out my hand. He stood and grasped it in both of his, gazing at me with eyes that were now mellow and liquid.

"I really do wish her well, Miss O'Neal. And you, too. I hope you find her."

I disengaged my hand, said a polite good-bye, and left, pulling the door back the way I had found it.

I retraced my steps down the hall and out the front door of the business administration building.

The day was warm and the campus was green and shiny with sunlight, just starting to fill with students scurrying to complete registration before classes started the following week. I walked north toward the lot behind the old gym where I had parked my Jeep, passing the library, an architectural freak with a sweep of concrete stairs and walls of tinted glass topped by a scalloped roof vaguely reminiscent of a pagoda. Someday I would have to find out how it got dropped, anomalously, amid the classic brick rectangles.

The parking meter had almost a half hour left. Good

luck for the student in the VW who trailed me to the space and waited patiently for me to back out.

The mail had arrived by the time I got home. An envelope from Curtis contained three photocopied memos, on plain paper, directed To: Whom It May Concern, From: Darla Hayden. Each had a scrawled *Darla* at the bottom, with the capital D turned into a smiling face.

The contents of the memos told a different story.

The first had been written more than a year ago. In language so formal she had to be aware of the irony, Darla Hayden informed the department faculty that, due to the regrettable but apparently unavoidable rupture in her relationship with her former committee chair, Aaron Hiller, she was in need of a new one. She had attempted to discuss this with him, but he had failed to meet her when she had set up an appointment through the department secretary. She offered her assurances of her willingness and ability to work with a new chair, without the entanglements she had previously experienced, especially if the new chair was willing to offer assurances in return that he wouldn't tell her he loved her and couldn't imagine his life without her, only to later insist that she had imagined the encounter.

I tried to imagine what it would feel like to make an appointment through a secretary in an attempt to see an ex-lover with veto power over your career. My stomach knotted.

The second memo was dated late January. In the same formal language, she was complaining that the professor who had been scheduled to teach a seminar on the Japanese financial markets, with special attention to yield curve risk in government bonds and yen interest rate derivatives, had never been less than thirty minutes late, had seldom stayed more than twenty minutes once there, and had failed to appear at all on four occasions. She asked the department to take formal action against the named professor, Gary Metzger.

That must have endeared her to all concerned. Professors cover for each other as tightly as doctors, lawyers, and senators, if not quite as religiously as cops.

The third memo, covering four, single-spaced, typewritten pages, was less than two months old. Darla Hayden was responding to word that she had failed her qualifying examination. She detailed the irregularities in exam procedure, including the university's failure to provide an operational computer with WordPerfect 5.2 for Windows, thus forcing her to choose between working with unfamiliar word-processing software or writing in longhand, an inefficient approach that kept her from fully displaying her knowledge in the area. Another detailed irregularity was the presence at the oral portion of her exams of the same Gary Metzger she had previously complained about, even though he was not a member of her committee, and his presence could only be imputed to spite. Metzger, she said, posed questions that he knew she could not possibly answer, because he had not covered them in the seminar where she could reasonably have been expected to learn them.

Shit. There she had been, surrounded by guys with rubber hoses, and she had hit them with her fists. She gave them reason to get her, and they got her. Now Thurman seemed to be worried they may have gotten her too hard—and maybe Hiller, too, although I wasn't sure at all how he felt. Certainly, Helen Stern thought Darla may have been hit too hard to recover.

Reading the memos, written in blood through Darla Hayden's tightly held, rigidly expressed pain, made me tired.

I hated everything that had happened between Darla and the university. As much as anything, I hated it because I had liked going to college, and I had wanted to think academia was a special world, one I had lived in for four years and could go back to if I chose. The relationship between Aaron Hiller and Darla Hayden, and the way the university treated her as a result, turned that into a lie.

At six o'clock I quit brooding about the case and watched the Channel 12 news, but I couldn't get past Brianne McKinley's popping eyes to hear the stories. I caught some visual about a bus accident that had "Tennessee" superimposed in the corner. I've never figured out why Tennessee bus accidents and Montana brushfires make the local news.

I thought about calling Curtis when it was over and didn't stop myself until I touched the phone. I could wait another twenty-four hours to ask what he really thought of his colleagues' behavior.

Besides, I had promised Deke a report of the day's activities. He'd be expecting me at the Mother Lode for dinner.

In fact, he hadn't waited for me. He was halfway through his steak when I slid onto the stool next to his at the counter of the Mother Lode coffee shop.

Diane brought me a beer and raised an eyebrow. A nod told her I wanted a hamburger. She reappeared with a plate almost immediately.

Deke chewed as I told him the story.

"So," he said when I was finished. "You think one of these professors might be in danger?"

"I don't know yet. But I'm feeling okay about not disclosing in so many words to Thurman that Darla Hayden might be thinking violent thoughts about him. I don't think it would have helped, and it might have hurt."

"Hurt who?"

"Darla, if she doesn't act and needs to talk to her therapist again. No confidence has been officially breached."

My hamburger had been sitting in front of me long enough that it was almost down to room temperature. I started in on it anyway.

"Sure is a lot of unofficial breaching going on." Deke pushed his plate away, something he should do more often. Soon he was going to need two stools. "Suppose she doesn't contact her therapist. How do you find her?"

"Not too many leads," I said, swallowing a little too quickly. I washed it down with beer. "The message on Thurman's computer may mean she hasn't gone far, though. I think I'll spend the day tomorrow checking places that rent rooms near the university, keeping an eye out for her car. And then see if I can find out anything more tomorrow evening."

"What happens then?"

"I go with Curtis to a faculty cocktail party." I said it as casually as I could. I didn't want Deke to feel I was holding out on him, which he would have if I hadn't told him until later.

"Yes. You can hear a lot at cocktail parties."

I turned to check the Keno board, and we let the subject drop. Deke left before I finished my hamburger, and I didn't bother to play a last Keno ticket.

The evening was saved when I got to bed with a beer and the cats just in time to hear Tex Ritter sing the opening theme to *High Noon*. I hung in with Grace Kelly until she and Gary Cooper shot Frank Miller dead, and I went to sleep at peace for a change, feeling there was justice in the world.

The feeling ebbed slightly the next day, when I couldn't find a trace of Darla Hayden in the cheap housing that attracts desperate students.

But I perked up while waiting for Curtis to pick me up for the cocktail party, even though I usually hate waiting, and I was apprehensive about the party. I was looking forward to seeing Curtis.

He was even five minutes early.

"I know you hate waiting," he said when I met him at the curb.

"Thanks." I nodded, and he smiled. I smiled back until I felt dumb.

He made a U-turn in his maroon Volvo and took a right on Mill, heading toward the freeway.

"Thanks for the memos, too," I added.

"What did you think of them?"

"I think everybody involved behaved pretty badly. On both sides."

"I think you're right."

"Does Hiller have a reputation for screwing students?"

Curtis hesitated while he negotiated his way onto 395 north.

"Aaron has a reputation for letting students down, for promising more than he delivers. He also has a reputation for encouraging students to work on research with him, only to forget to include their names when the research is published. When he was younger, he was rumored to be a womanizer. And his current wife was his student when he divorced his first wife. But if he became involved with a student other than Darla Hayden in the five years since he came to UNR, it isn't public knowledge."

"How does this guy stay respected?"

"I don't know how to answer that." Curtis seldom admitted he didn't know how to answer something, and I was almost sorry I asked. Especially since he was frowning as he cloverleafed to 80 west. "He publishes a lot, even if he doesn't write all of it, and his early work made a real contribution to the field. Besides, he's good with the media, and he has tenure."

"Oh, Curtis. You make it all sound so lousy, the university *danse macabre*."

"Sometimes it is that. I still think it's better than any other dance I could do—or than most people do."

We rode the rest of the way in silence. He parked by the old gym, on the faculty side of the lot, not the metered side where I had been the day before. We walked together, still silent, down the path to the student union, and around to the concrete deck overlooking Manzanita Lake with the glass doors that marked the faculty center entrance.

The space was too large for the few people who had showed up so far. They had clustered around the bar, at the far corner from the entrance. Besides being the tallest two people in the room, we were the only two in jeans, and for me it was a long walk. Curtis didn't seem conscious of it, but I felt my paranoia level rise with every step.

Especially since Randolph Thurman and Aaron Hiller, with two women surely their wives, were standing slightly to the right of the small group, staring at Curtis and me. Hiller was shorter than Curtis, but outweighed him by maybe twenty pounds of muscle.

"You're drinking beer?" Curtis asked.

"Yes. Thanks."

I shifted as far to the left as I could while he got drinks for us. I tried not to stare back at Thurman and Hiller, but my eyes kept swerving in that direction.

Curtis and I had evidently been the beginning of a rolling wave of arrivals. More men and women in business suits, and a couple in his-and-hers sport jackets, were filling in behind him at the bar, blocking the access, visual or otherwise, from left to right. I wasn't exactly relaxed when he handed me my beer, but the paranoia had eased a little.

He introduced me to the nearest quartet, including the couple dressed alike, and I smiled and nodded and didn't try to participate in the conversation.

Nobody asked what I did for a living. So far, so good.

A student came around with a tray of chicken nuggets, followed by another with a tray of cheese and crackers. I helped myself, figuring a full mouth would further discourage questions. In fact, the people Curtis introduced me to seemed perfectly happy talking to him about the fall class schedule and ignoring me.

I got myself a second beer and retreated before Aaron Hiller could work his way toward me. He kept coming, though.

"Aaron!" Curtis said brightly. "I think you've met Freddie."

"I have had the pleasure. But I wasn't aware that she's a friend of yours," Aaron replied, echoing the light tone Curtis had used.

"I don't often mix my business life with my personal one," I said. "I didn't think to mention that I'd be here tonight."

"Let me assure you that I understand." Aaron flashed the amazingly intimate smile, so that I would feel especially assured. Without missing a beat, he aimed the flash at Curtis. "You've taken a great leap upward in my estimation, Breckinridge. I didn't know you had the judgment to mix business and pleasure with such an interesting and unusual woman."

I started to bristle, but Curtis laughed.

"Give me a call when you want to talk about judgment," he said.

Aaron patted him on the shoulder without losing his smile.

"We'll talk." He nodded to the four horrified people who had been part of the original conversation and moved gracefully away.

"That was brave, Curtis," one of the men said. "But

somebody ought to talk to you about judgment. You won't make full professor until Aaron retires."

"If then," a woman added. "He'll probably put it in his will—a hefty bequest to the university, as long as Curtis Breckinridge never receives another merit raise or promotion."

"Curtis teaches leadership," I said. "And good leaders have integrity. Sometimes it's important for professors to practice what they teach."

"Just what is your business?" the second man asked.

I was aware of a silence creeping across the room in our direction.

"I'm a private investigator," I replied, just before the silence reached us.

Everyone had turned toward the entrance to the room.

A young woman was standing just inside the glass doors, looking from group to group, from face to face. Her frizzy dark hair had escaped from a clip and fallen down one side of her pale face. The blue jeans and UNR sweatshirt might have come from the student store.

But she must have bought the semiautomatic somewhere else.

The gun was braced loosely against her hip, so she wasn't planning to open fire in a hurry. I began easing my way to the back of the crowds, then started toward her left, the side away from the gun.

"I just want to talk," she said loudly. Her voice was high-pitched and nervous. "I'm not threatening anybody."

"Then please put the gun down, Darla."

The voice was Randolph Thurman's. He moved to the front of the group. A small man with unexpected courage.

"I'm not putting it down until I get an apology," Darla said, still searching faces.

"What is it you want me to say?" Thurman asked.

"Not just you. That's why I'm here. I want one from every professor who shot me down. But we can start with you."

"Fine. I handled the situation badly. As department chair, I should have stepped in earlier. What else do you want me to say?"

By the time I had worked my way as close to Darla as I could get without breaking free of the group, I had realized there was something else wrong with the way she was holding the gun. Her hand was slack, as if the gun had no weight.

"She's not threatening you," I called to Thurman. "She's not holding a loaded gun."

Darla whirled around.

"Who are you?"

"Somebody who doesn't want you hurt," I said. "And waving a gun—even an unloaded gun—at a roomful of frightened people is a good way to get yourself killed."

"So what?"

The eyes that met mine were haunted and despairing.

"So let's go somewhere and call Helen Stern."

That stunned her. And I don't know what she would have answered, if three men hadn't rushed her from the other side.

Darla screamed as she landed on the floor, two of them on top of her.

"It's a fucking toy," the third man, the one who had grabbed the gun, said. "It's a fucking toy."

Darla kept screaming, and the rest of the room was abuzz with noise and movement.

I found myself somehow next to Randolph Thurman.

"You still don't have to call the police," I said. "She hasn't done anything that can't be explained."

He shook his head. "Too late. Aaron went to call them while I was talking to her."

We both heard the siren as he spoke.

# Chapter 4

"BRIANNE WANTS TO interview you," Curtis said when he called the next afternoon.

I was going to have to think about that. I could add it to the list.

One of the police officers who had responded to Aaron Hiller's phone call was Michelle Urrutia, cousin of the Elko police chief, a friend of mine from Reno High days. I explained as much as of the situation to her as I could, and while they still took Darla Hayden in, Michelle helped me argue for booking her on a single charge of disturbing the peace. Michelle couldn't promise it would end that way, and I wouldn't have asked her to.

The Channel 12 news crew got there just as Michelle was hustling Darla into the black and white. An earnest-looking field reporter with a cowlick in his otherwise smooth brown hair didn't have to search for an interviewee. Aaron Hiller was standing next to him, smiling his professional smile, by the time the camera was running.

I sort of recognized Aaron's version of events, although he made Darla Hayden sound more unbalanced and threatening than I thought was necessary. On the other hand, that made the rest of us—especially Randolph Thurman and me—sound like stand-ins for Sylvester Stallone.

Curtis insisted that we stay until the crew packed up, because observing it was arguably connected with his consulting job. The reporter recognized him and got a brief statement that wasn't nearly as jazzy as Aaron's, even if it was closer to what had happened.

I did my best to hide whenever the camera appeared to be panning in my direction. I've never been able to figure out why some people want so desperately to be on television. I've always seen it as an opportunity to make a fool of yourself in front of thousands of people who would otherwise never have an excuse to accost you at the grocery store and tell you what they think of you.

It was almost midnight by the time we left the campus.

"What do you want to do now?" Curtis asked as he maneuvered the maroon Volvo out of the parking lot and turned south on Virginia Street.

"Figure out how to salvage Darla Hayden. But it isn't my job, and I don't know how to do it anyway."

He shot a quick glance and a half-smile at me.

"I was thinking more along the lines of coffee or a drink."

"No noise or crowds."

"What about my place? It isn't far."

I realized—I knew it, but I hadn't thought about it—that I'd never seen Curtis's place.

"Sure. That would be fine."

The faculty cocktail party was supposed to be one small step in the relationship. I had liked being with Curtis, and I had been impressed with the way he handled both Aaron Hiller and the television crew. Going to Curtis's place meant looking at the possibility of even another step. And I knew I wasn't ready to take it.

"Maybe not," I added.

"Which is it? Fine or not?" He braked the car so that he could look at me.

A young man on the well-lit lawn of the Delta Phi house was shouting up at a sister on the second floor, who was shouting back down at him.

"Can't we just talk?" he yelled.

"Noooo," she wailed. "Go awaaay."

A buddy was tugging at the young man's arm. He fell to his knees, sobbing.

"Let's go, man," the buddy said.

"Noooo," the young man echoed.

Curtis was still waiting for an answer.

"I'd like to see your place," I said carefully, "but not tonight. I'd like to see it when I drive over in my own car and don't have to ask you to drive me home."

"That's fair enough. Although I didn't plan on attacking you." He accelerated away from the sorority house scene.

"I'm sorry. That came out as if I don't trust you. And I do. In a lot of ways." I hoped he wouldn't ask me to name them, not right then. "And I was really proud of you tonight."

"Proud of me?"

"Yeah."

"That's funny—I was proud of you, too."

The tensions eased a little. We rode in silence until he had picked up the freeway, first east and then south to the Mill exit.

"Would you rather I just dropped you off?" he asked.

"I guess it won't surprise you if I say I'm not sure what I want," I answered.

"No. It won't. And I'm not sure what I can say that will help."

"That has to be rough," I said.

He laughed.

"It is." He stopped the car in front of my house, letting the engine idle. He turned toward me again, or at least as well as he could within the restraints of the seat belt. "How's this? You're a puzzle solver. If you can figure out what you need me to say, so that you can stop being scared that I'm going to take off and leave you as soon as you start thinking you might care, I'll try to say it. As long as you remember that life doesn't come with guarantees."

"That's pretty good, Curtis. That's pretty good." I unbuckled myself so that I could kiss him good night properly. His mouth was firm and smooth. I was surprised at how good it felt. "And I promise I'll think about it."

"I'll call you tomorrow," he said, attempting to kiss me back.

"Okay." That was the best I could do. I slid out of the car.

Sundance was glad to see me, but Butch waited until the Volvo was out of sight, thumping his full gray tail on the porch, before he followed us in. He sulked with his back to me until there was food in two dishes and Sundance was eating, and even then he only nibbled.

"That isn't going to work," I told him. "I don't believe you'll go on a hunger strike, not from jealousy or anything else. So you might as well cut it out now."

His ears went back, but he didn't turn around. And he ate it all, I discovered when I checked later.

I got into bed and stared at the dark ceiling.

What did I want from Curtis? And if I wanted something substantial—as at least part of me did—what could he say that would make me think it was okay to go after it?

Sundance hopped up on the bed and made himself comfortable on the spare pillow, then proceeded to slurp his own ass, tail tickling my cheek. Butch slipped in next to my chest, purring. Everything as usual.

I tried to imagine how different it would be if Curtis were here. And I didn't know how to start.

Sex would be the obvious place, but sex just seemed like a complicating factor to me. I'm not really the type of person who gets swept away by passion. Or at least I haven't been very often. I tried to imagine how it would feel to wake up in the morning and find Curtis there. I'd probably bury my face in the pillow, hope he made good coffee, and pray he wouldn't ask me to talk before I'd had a cup. That was as far as I could go.

So I thought about Darla Hayden instead.

I wondered what she had believed—really—that she would get from Aaron Hiller. But I hit a dead end there, too.

I have a limited number of ways to deal with sleepless nights. A few stretching exercises, a hot bath and a beer, a channel surf for something truly numbing on television. Fortunately, I was tired enough that the hot bath with a beer did it.

The phone call from Curtis wasn't the first one I got the next day. Sandra Herrick, a friend who is also a reporter for the Nevada *Herald*, beat him to it. So did my mother. The story had made both the late news and the morning paper.

I told them both the same thing—that there was nothing to tell.

"A graduate student threatened a roomful of professors with a toy gun. You were there. You have to have something to tell," Sandra said. "And if you won't tell me that story, I want to know what's going on with your own personal professor. Is it serious yet?"

"Okay. I'd rather talk about the graduate student. She feels they treated her badly and she wanted them to pay attention. She wanted them to regret flunking her out."

"Well, she got attention. But I can't imagine it helped her cause."

"No. I guess not."

"Was she really sleeping with Aaron Hiller?"

"He doesn't deny it."

"You'd think the word would get around, but he still seems to score."

"What do you mean? I heard she was his only lapse of fidelity since he's been in Reno."

"That might be the line on campus, but not in town. He's rumored to have privately tutored several women.

The latest is supposed to be Brianne McKinley, the Channel 12 anchor."

"No shit." Add that to the list of things to think about. "That's going on now?"

"So I hear. Does it matter?"

"I don't know. Probably not. Anything else I should know?"

"Lunch next week. I'll trade you everything I know for everything you know. But that includes what's-his-name. Curtis? Is that it?"

"That's it. See you."

I could take the few days to sort out what I wanted Sandra to know.

My mother accepted my protestation of ignorance about the student, and I immediately wished I hadn't lied to her.

"When can you and the professor—Curtis?—come up for dinner? He looks so nice, and Al and I are dying to meet him," she cooed. Ramona coos when she wants me to do something.

"I'll have to get back to you on that. I'm not ready to invite him to meet my mother." And especially not my stepfather. I don't get along with Ramona's husband, Al, and I couldn't conceive of a pleasant dinner for four, not even at Lake Tahoe.

"But you think you might be soon, I can tell from your voice."

"Wrong. This will take a while. Maybe a long time. I don't want you to worry about it."

"I'm not worried about it. Although I do worry about you—I want you to be happy."

"I don't want to have this conversation now," I snapped. Not a good idea. Snapping at Ramona is never a good idea.

"That's fine, dear. Let me know when you want to talk. And let me know next time you're on the news—we don't usually stay up to watch it, you know. We were lucky that we caught you and your friend. And it does embarrass Al when other people tell him what you've been doing, you know that."

Al was a state assemblyman, a position of great importance in Ramona's fantasies.

"I'm sorry. I'll call. I promise. Good-bye."

I ended the conversation a little too abruptly, but I wanted to get off the phone before she snapped back at me. And I frankly don't give a damn whether Al is embarrassed or not. And I don't like feeling guilty when she argues that I should have called.

I needed a walk to cool off, and I wanted to find out what had happened to Darla Hayden. I took the two blocks to the police station in long, loping strides.

The desk sergeant, Danny Sinclair, was not a friend of mine, but I asked for an update on Darla Hayden anyway.

"She's outta here," he said with a malicious grin. "Got bailed out an hour ago."

"Bailed out?"

"A misdemeanor disturbing-the-peace was the only charge. No reason to keep her."

"Who bailed her out? Where did she go?"

"Is that your business?"

"Well, yeah, it is." I exhaled sharply with annoyance. "I need to find her. I was hired to find her, in fact."

"She has a court date for Tuesday. Try then."

"I've been hired on a collection case, and she isn't supposed to have any money. Tell me who bailed her out. I'll owe you."

"And I'll never collect, because you don't have anything I want."

I hated his blotchy, freckled face and his yellow teeth. "Please."

He made a big show of pulling the file up on the computer.

"Helen Stern. That's the name. And that's all you get."

"Damn. That's all?"

He seemed delighted that I wanted more.

"That's all."

I got back home just as annoyed as I was when I left.

And then Curtis called, to say Brianne wanted to interview me.

"About what?" I asked. "Last night? I don't know anything everyone else doesn't know."

"Have you had a bad morning?"

"Yes. Darla Hayden got out of jail before I had a chance to talk to her. And I argued for a reduced charge, and the shrink bailed her out, and what am I going to do if she disappears again?"

"Blame yourself, of course. What else has happened?"

I almost laughed. "Of course. And nothing else worth mentioning. What exactly does Brianne want?"

"She'd like to tape an interview Monday morning, then edit it down for about two minutes to show on the news."

I almost asked what I got out of it, then realized that I

wanted to meet Brianne. No professional reason, but I was curious, both because I'd watched her on television and because Sandra had said she was sleeping with Aaron Hiller.

"Did she tell you what time and where?"

"Eleven A.M. at the studio. Will you do it?" He sounded surprised.

"I'll show up at eleven and see what she plans to ask. How's that?"

"More than I expected." He paused for so long that I thought it must be my turn to say something, but then he started again before I found words. "Do you want to have dinner tonight?"

"I think I'll look for Deke tonight. He'll be annoyed if I don't tell him the story personally."

"Is that something I could do with you? I'd like to meet Deke, if it wouldn't make you uncomfortable."

In truth, it would make me uncomfortable, and Curtis surely knew it. And he could argue that if he could take me to a faculty party, I could take him to the Mother Lode. On the other hand, I still didn't have an answer to his question, what he could say to help me feel secure enough to get involved.

"I'd like to do that sometime," I said. "Not yet."

"Okay. Let me know."

"Will you be at the television station Monday morning?"

"Probably. I'll make that yes."

"Lunch, then."

"See you."

Curtis was a nice man. I hoped I wasn't screwing up.

I tried to call Deke, but I got his machine. Normally, I wouldn't have bothered to even try. I would have wandered to the Mother Lode for dinner, expecting him to be there. It was just that I'd used him as an excuse. Well, he'd either show up at the Mother Lode or not. I'd done what I could.

I was still restless and edgy when I got off the phone. Sooner or later I would have to talk to Helen Stern. Since I had found Darla Hayden—or she had found me, anyway—and the collection agency could pick it up from here, the case was pretty much wrapped up.

But I couldn't quite leave it alone. Bailing Darla out had to be breaking through the therapeutic borders big time, and I wondered why she had done it. Her office was a pleasant afternoon walk away, and the trek would do me good.

Taking Wheeler to Virginia, then doglegging to Court, meant I stayed south of the Truckee River and away from the worst of the casino area, the part that was starting to look more like old downtown Las Vegas every day— tiny, dirty pawnshops and dusty, fake souvenir shops sandwiched between considerably larger, decaying gambling establishments.

The corporate-owned monsters—Bally's and the MGM Grand—were a tentative start to a Reno Strip well away from the residential area. But this part of the city, from Wingfield Park to Virginia Lake and west to Reno High, looked the same as it always had, all my life. I wouldn't have been surprised to find that people living behind the hedges and the circular driveways, the ones with the old rose bushes, still thought Eisenhower was president.

Even so, there was something comforting to me about the shade trees and Victorian homes on Court Street. I wondered if that was why they were all medical office buildings now—to lull the patient's anxiety.

Helen Stern had that same sign on her door, the one telling me to come in and be seated. Seeing clients on a Saturday fit with what little I knew about her.

I went into the library and looked for the book about Freud and women again, but I couldn't find it. Maybe clients who had to wait got borrowing privileges.

I picked up a paperback which promised to tell me how to maintain my own identity in a relationship and sat down in the armchair. Helen Stern came out of her office, and I heard her voice saying good-bye to someone before I had a chance to get past the exclamation points on the cover. I put the book back with a small twinge of reluctance.

"You could call before coming," she said when she saw me. Her eyelids still had that bruised look, but the irises seemed clearer, the pupils more focused. And this time her clothes matched—a tunic and pants of un-bleached cotton, with red embroidery on the cuffs.

"I thought you'd expect me."

"Let's say I'm not surprised." She stepped back out of the doorway, and I followed her into her office.

We settled into the same chairs, same positions, as we had the week before. I had an uncomfortable sense of what therapy might be like.

"Why'd you bail her out?" I asked.

"Because she called me. Because she didn't have anyone else to call. And I didn't want her to stay in jail."

The light from the window made a halo of her frizzy gray hair. "She was very upset, you know, when you mentioned my name in the faculty center. I did my best to reassure her that no confidence had been breached, that I was only concerned for her, but I'm not certain she believed me. Bailing her out was also a way of demonstrating my confidence in her."

"Suppose she doesn't show up on Tuesday?"

"Then my confidence will have been misplaced, and she'll owe me more money. But she promised me she would be there, and Darla doesn't break promises."

I shook my head.

"I'm no therapist, but the woman I saw last night with that toy gun didn't look rational enough to remember what promises are."

"She's overwrought, I agree. In fact, I made bail conditional on Darla'a agreeing to resume therapy."

"Good luck with that." I was trying to figure out how this woman could be so smart and so gullible at the same time. I also had to consider that I hadn't seen Darla Hayden at her best. "Did you at least get an address?"

"Yes, but I'm afraid I can't give it to you. I'll call the collection agency on Monday, tell them I've changed my mind. I'll pay them for their trouble and for your time."

I shook my head again. "Dr. Stern, I went out on a limb last night, arguing that Darla Hayden hadn't committed much of a crime. In fact, she scared the hell out of a bunch of people, most of whom didn't deserve it." The way she leaned back in her chair and blinked made me realize that I had shouted at her. I lowered my voice. "I agree with you, that jail isn't the place for her. But I'm not happy that she's running around loose, either."

"So what do you want to do, Ms. O'Neal? I made the best decision I could. Can you make a better one?"

She leaned forward again, eyebrows raised, head tilted quizzically.

"If you're mocking me, I can do without the sarcasm." I stood up. "I'll call the collection agency Monday, too. I'll tell them that once she was arrested, I was off the job."

"I'll see you out," she said. "I am grateful for the effort you made, both the effort to find Darla and the effort to see that she wasn't charged with a felony. I heard the story when I went to the police station this morning."

She held out her hand, and I took it. The skin was leathery, as if she worked in her garden without gloves.

"I hope Darla shows up on Tuesday," I said.

"Good luck on your next case," Helen Stern replied.

# Chapter 5

MAKEUP. I HADN'T thought about makeup. But when I reached the squat concrete building on McCarran Boulevard that housed the television station, the receptionist led me neither to Brianne McKinley's desk, which was where I thought we were going, nor to some small studio for taping. Instead, we went straight to the makeup room. I was sitting on a high stool in front of a mirror staring at my freckles before I had time to protest.

A man in his thirties, wearing an open-necked khaki shirt, interposed himself between me and the glass. I could see the bald spot in his curly brown hair bobbing back and forth as he looked down his nose at my pores.

"Do we have to do this?" I asked.

"You want to do this," he answered. "Otherwise, you'd look pasty and unsympathetic on camera. I won't turn you into a different person. I'll just smooth out the color of your skin and pick up your eyes. You have interesting eyes, but they're hard to notice without a touch of liner and mascara. And you shouldn't have worn a striped shirt. Didn't anyone tell you not to wear a striped shirt?"

"I didn't ask."

He rubbed a small triangle of sponge over some pancake base and started daubing my cheeks.

"Narrow white stripes shimmer on television. They distract from your face."

"I'll remember for next time." I meant it as a joke, but he nodded.

"And remember to wear warm colors. Warm colors will bring out your own natural attractiveness. Peachy tones, corals. Stay away from the dark reds and the violets." He brushed a pale rouge lightly over my cheeks, chin, and the tip of my nose. "Brianne doesn't have the same tones in her skin, but I'd still suggest that you borrow a blouse from her for the interview. If size isn't a problem, too."

"That's okay. For two minutes, I can shimmer." I hadn't met her, and I didn't want to borrow her blouse. And I was certain size would be a problem.

"Close your eyes. I know two minutes doesn't sound like much to you, but it's a long time when the camera is running. Now look up."

I did as I was told. I could feel the brief swipe of eye shadow, then the short strokes of the eyebrow pencil and liner. His breath smelled of chewing gum over coffee.

I flinched when I saw the mascara wand heading toward my cornea.

"Do you want to do it yourself?" he asked.

"No. You might as well finish." I tried to focus beyond his hands. Surely, if he had ever blinded someone, he would have been fired.

"There." He stepped away from the mirror. "What do you think?"

I looked as if I were wearing a mask. Still, I could recognize everything but the eyes.

"I think I look like Nefertiti with long blond hair."

He frowned. "Nefertiti had a narrow face and a small chin. You don't. And I didn't do that much to your eyes. I think you look gorgeous."

"Thank you. I guess I'm not used to gorgeous."

"Try." He patted me on the shoulder.

"Is she ready?"

The enthusiastic voice startled me. Brianne was next to the chair before I knew it.

"Yes, except for the shirt. We need to find one she can wear on camera. Does Lane have a spare? She's about his size."

"Be a dear and check." The makeup man nodded and slipped away. Brianne focused her popping eyes and intimate smile on my reflection in the mirror. Her yellow blazer was so bright that no one was going to notice me no matter what I wore. "I'm so glad you could make it on such short notice. And don't be nervous. We're just going to have a good time. I'm going to ask you to tell me a little about what you do and then some specific questions about the incident at the university Friday night. Everyone was so lucky that you happened to be there with Curtis."

I tried to come up with something smart to say about that.

"What do you think?"

The makeup man was back with a light-blue shirt on a hanger. He held it out for Brianne to inspect.

"Perfect." She removed it from the hanger and held it under my chin. "We'll wait outside while you change."

They were gone in an instant, and I was left with the shirt. It was soft, the kind of cotton that has been refined until it feels almost like silk. And the blue was as warm as a baby's blanket. I tossed my brown-and-white striped Western shirt over the back of the makeup chair and put it on. I was still tucking it into my jeans when I heard a man shouting in the hall.

"I don't care who she is, or what a coup it is to interview her. You're supposed to let me know, in advance, when you want to schedule something for the evening news. I didn't approve this!"

"If I waited for your approval every time I had an idea, our ratings would be so low we'd all be editing copy in Winnemucca!" That was Brianne's voice.

The decibel level dropped. I didn't want to open the door on that scene, so I waited until I was fairly sure the voices wouldn't rise again.

Curtis was alone in the hallway when I stepped out.

"How did you do it?" I asked.

He opened his mouth to answer, but his jaw hung suspended. His eyes were so wide they would have shamed John Barrymore.

"Wow," he finally said.

"Wow, what?" I tried to back into the makeup room, but he grabbed my hand.

"I'm sorry. I don't want to make you nervous." His jaw and eyes both returned to normal. "You look terrific. I'm just going to drop you off at the taping room. When you're through, we'll have lunch."

I pulled my hand back. "One more time. 'Wow.' Wow, what?"

"An involuntary reaction." He paused to let the professorial side take control. "From the first evening, I was attracted to your mind, your sense of humor, and a quality best described as guts. I simply hadn't realized—and it's my problem, not yours—how much I am attracted to you physically."

"Until somebody made me up like Playmate of the Month."

"That's not what you look like at all. Come on. Brianne's waiting."

He held out his hand. I almost didn't take it.

"Okay."

I let him usher me down the hall. I still wanted to know how he ended the shouting, but I was too annoyed to ask again. He opened a door marked C and walked away before I even got inside.

A tall, thin, coffee-colored man wearing a cordless headset grabbed my arm and whisked me to a swivel chair made of molded gray plastic. Facing it was another of the same amorphous ilk. A small table was in between. The wall behind us was masked with black curtains.

The area with the chairs and table was lit by a row of bright lights hanging from the ceiling. I made the mistake of looking up at them, and then I couldn't see the rest of the room.

"Great shirt," the man said. "Lane has a bunch just like it."

He ignored my glare and retrieved a tiny microphone draped over one wing of the chair.

"We need to run the cord inside your shirt and clip the head to your collar. You can slip it beneath the button closest to your waist."

I felt like an FBI informant. Once I was wired and clipped, he sat me down.

"When the red light is on, so is the camera." There were two cameras in the room. My eyes had recovered enough so that I could pick them out. He pointed to one of them. "That one is focused on you. The other one is Brianne's. She'll open the interview. Either camera can pull back for a two-shot. Any questions?"

Before I could answer, Brianne plopped into the opposite chair. She slid the microphone wire inside her blazer and clipped the head to her lapel in one smooth movement.

She smiled at me with the same intimacy I had felt in my living room.

"Ready?"

"Sure."

"I'll introduce the edited clip from the anchor's desk, so we're not going to tape an intro now. I'll just start with the first question."

"Okay."

Brianne looked at the coffee-colored man. He nodded and pointed to her camera. The red light went on. She looked toward me, earnestly.

"As a licensed private investigator, what kind of work do you do?"

"Mostly skip-trace. People who don't pay bills, who

disappear owing somebody something. Sometimes I do legal work, too." I added that because I wanted to impress her. I was immediately sorry. It made me aware of how insecure I was.

"Legal work? Attorneys hire you?" She leaned forward, as if I had succeeded in impressing her after all.

"Yeah. The police do a good job, but lawyers will sometimes want some extra work done, especially if they feel the police have closed the case too quickly."

I relaxed a little, but I hoped she wouldn't pursue that. I thought I was fortunate when she didn't.

"You're the only female private investigator in Reno. Is that an advantage?"

Out of the corner of my eye, I caught a finger pointing toward my camera. The red light went on.

"I don't know. Some people think so."

"You were in the university faculty center Friday night when Darla Hayden, a doctoral student who flunked her comprehensive examinations last spring, threatened her former adviser with what turned out to be a toy gun. Some people credit you with defusing a potentially dangerous situation, even though the gun wasn't real. Was that a coincidence?"

"What?"

"What were you doing in the faculty center Friday night?"

I couldn't figure out why that felt like a loaded question. The lights were too hot, and I was starting to perspire in Lane Josten's shirt.

"One of the professors is a friend of mine, and he had asked me to the party."

"That's all?"

"Yeah."

"But isn't it true that you had been on campus just the day before, asking questions about Darla Hayden?"

"Well, yeah." Damn. The Aaron Hiller connection.

"And didn't you catch Darla Hayden off guard Friday night by mentioning the name of her therapist?"

"I shouldn't have done that."

"Did Darla Hayden's therapist hire you to collect a bill?"

I was beginning to feel as if a good hound dog had my scent, and I had to start another trail.

"I'm not going to answer that question. Besides, isn't it true you have this information because you're sleeping with Aaron Hiller?"

Brianne's body jerked back. I could see her mind working as her mouth tried to form a follow-up question.

A laugh came through a speaker somewhere near the ceiling. A male voice—the same one I had heard shouting in the hall—called, "She's got you!"

"Do you ever feel ashamed of what you do, Ms. O'Neal?" Brianne asked sweetly.

"Do you?" I countered.

"I think we'll end this for now," she said. "But I may ask for a rematch."

She turned to look at the camera. I followed her gaze and realized that the red light had been on the whole time.

"Stop the tape and kill the lights," she said. The smile clicked off.

The red light blinked out, and so did the hot lights,

although it was too late to save the shirt. Recessed fluorescents cast a harsh glow on the room.

"This wasn't a contest," I said. "And I don't want to do it again."

I realized there had been a person attached to each camera. Two young men peered curiously as the man with the headset unclipped my microphone. Brianne unclipped her own and draped it over the side of the chair.

"I'll tell your friend you're available for lunch." She left the room without looking back.

"That was great!" A slim man with wiry black hair and matching mustache trotted up to me. He had come in through another door, one next to a large window. "I'm Steve Burns."

I shook the outstretched hand.

"Freddie O'Neal."

"That was great," he repeated, chuckling. "That's the first time I've ever seen Brianne speechless on camera. She goes after people, and they usually just take it. I wish we could use that shot of her face."

"You won't?"

"Not till she works for someone else, I'm afraid. Can't undermine our own anchor's credibility." He was clearly unhappy at being forced into that position.

"Will you use any of the interview?"

"Probably just a few seconds—a shot of you to illustrate an update on the Hayden story, something like that." He smiled to let me know it was nothing personal.

"Okay." I was actually relieved. Living the interview had been bad enough. I could do without the replay.

"Could you help me find the makeup room? I left a shirt there. And I'll have this one cleaned before I return it to Lane."

"Don't be silly. We'll have it cleaned. Put your own shirt back on and just leave this one in the makeup room."

He took my elbow and led me into the hall. I tried to disengage, but his grip was firm.

"The makeup room is the second door, the one that's open."

"Thanks. And how do I find Curtis Breckinridge?"

Steve Burns's face lit up with an impish glow. "He was watching. He'll find you."

Shit. I hoped I hadn't messed up Curtis's consulting job. I hadn't thought of that.

"Tell him I'll be right out."

The makeup room was empty. I glanced at my unfamiliar self in the mirror and considered wiping my face clean. What the hell. I could look gorgeous through lunch.

My shirt was where I had left it. I was actually glad I hadn't been wearing it for the interview—it felt good to change into something dry.

Curtis was in the hall when I came out.

"Did I screw up?" I asked.

"Well—let's say it was a learning experience for Brianne. And for me, too. I wish you'd said something to me about Brianne and Aaron before blurting it on camera, though. Even if it wasn't live."

We both knew I would have done the same thing if it had been. I hadn't even thought about the difference.

"I didn't mean to cause problems for you. I only heard about their affair Saturday. I didn't have a chance to tell you."

"It's okay." His smile was a little off-center. "If you're ready, let's go."

We had reached the front door when Steve Burns caught up with us.

"Curtis, I thought you might want to know—we're sending Mark Martin and a camera crew to the university." He clapped a friendly hand on Curtis's shoulder.

I remembered Mark Martin—the young man with the cowlick who had been there Friday night.

"What's up?" Curtis asked, frowning.

"A group of graduate students are passing out flyers in support of Darla Hayden. They're asking everyone to gather in the quad at one."

Curtis turned to me. "Do you want to check it out?"

"Sure, why not? Lunch can wait." I was hungry, but I was curious, too. And this would give us something to talk about other than my behavior.

We drove separate cars. I followed his Volvo, and was only slightly annoyed when Curtis took Oddie east to 395 and then took 80 west to the university. Cutting across on Wells Avenue would have been shorter. Next time he could follow me.

Curtis pulled into the faculty lot behind the gym, and I found a spot at one of the meters. He waited while I fished for quarters.

The campus seemed to be functioning as usual, some students wandering north toward Fine Arts, some wandering south toward the student union or the business school. We crossed in front of the library to the quad.

A few students were standing by the statue of John Mackay, looking around. Nothing else was happening.

"Some event," I said.

"It isn't one o'clock yet. We could leave and come back," Curtis replied.

A male student wearing a plaid shirt and jeans waved at someone behind us, then trotted in our direction. I turned to see Mark Martin and a cameraman. The three met at the edge of the grass.

"Thanks for coming," the student said. "We've been waiting for you. If you could set up the camera by the statue, I'd like to make a statement."

"Sure," Mark said. He nodded to Curtis and me.

The student led him away.

"Why is he doing this?" I asked Curtis. "A handful of disgruntled students can't be news."

"Maybe, maybe not. He'll tape the statement because he's here. That doesn't mean they'll use it."

Someone with a book bag jostled my elbow. I turned to see a scraggly line of students forming a meandering trail that stretched from the news van to the quad. The cameraman as Pied Piper. Slowly, students began to collect around the statue. The man in the plaid shirt waited for the camera to get an establishing shot of the quad and the group before he started to speak.

"We are gathered here in support of Darla Hayden," he announced. "While her situation may be extreme, the pressures that drove her to desperation are not that far from the ones that each of us must cope with, usually alone."

"Who's the guy with the mission?" I whispered.

"I don't know him," Curtis whispered back. "I don't think he belongs to the business school."

"Graduate students are treated no better than indentured servants by the professors who hold their futures in a death grip. For little more than slave wages, we teach the classes, and we do the research. They take the credit. They build their careers on our backs. We cannot fight separately, or we will all be Darla Haydens. We must fight as a group." Despite the words, the student was plainly delivering the speech to the camera, not the group in front of the statue.

"Do you really want to stay for this?" I kept my voice low.

"A little longer. He has a point—and the offenses against graduate students here are mild compared with what happens at some of the major research universities. If you except Darla Hayden." Curtis was still watching the orator.

"Then you do think she was sinned against?"

"We'll talk about it later."

"Today we meet on campus. Tomorrow morning, we meet at the courthouse. We will be there every day Darla Hayden is there. She fought back alone. From now on, we must fight back with her." The student raised his arms like a champion boxer. But the crowd didn't cheer.

Mark Martin had been holding his microphone out to pick up the speech. Now he took it back and turned to the camera. He spoke so quietly I couldn't hear what he was saying. The students began to disperse, and the camera caught their backs, walking away.

"Okay," Curtis said. "That's enough. Do you want to go somewhere else for lunch or will the faculty center do?"

"I'm not sure I want to go to the faculty center again quite so soon."

"Curtissss! Curtissss!"

The name came out in something like a stage whisper, like the ghost of Hamlet's father. We both looked around for the source.

"Curtisss! Curtisss! Over here!"

Randolph Thurman was waving from an open window in the corner of the business administration building.

He slunk back as we approached.

"Curtis," he whispered again. "You have to get rid of the camera!"

"What's wrong, Randy?"

Thurman's face was white and sweaty, as if he had just finished losing his lunch.

"Darla Hayden," he whispered. "I found her body in Aaron's office. She was murdered!"

# Chapter 6

SOME PEOPLE GET used to death. Surgeons, coroners, undertakers, hit men, all those who watch the transition or traffic with the aftermath, must get used to seeing the lump of decaying, flesh-covered organs that lived as a human being before the cataclysm severed body and soul. I have yet to develop a callus over the place in my heart that automatically mourns the loss, the individual loss, each time.

Looking at Darla Hayden's body, curled in a fetal position on the industrial gray carpet between Aaron Hiller's desk and sofa, was more difficult even than other such sights had been. Not that I have seen that many, and none have been easy. But I remembered with a distinct twinge of guilt that if it hadn't been for my intervention, she might be sitting safely in a jail cell.

On top of that, the ugly purple bruises on her face meant that she was probably beaten badly before she died. What wasn't easy for me had been a whole hell of a lot worse for her.

"You have to call the police," I said to Thurman. "Now."

"Just another few minutes." He was still glued to the office window. "Curtis is shaking hands with the reporter. I'll call as soon as the news van is out of sight."

"What the hell good is that going to do? They'll pick up the report from the police radio and be right back. If they see the black-and-white, they'll even follow it. Forget about losing the van."

I wanted to shake the cowardly son of a bitch. I would have called the police myself, but I didn't want to use the phone in Hiller's office, and I didn't want to leave the crime scene. Thurman could have messed it up already, I knew that. Still, I felt better keeping tabs on Darla's body until someone else arrived. Besides, if I asked a secretary for a phone, I'd have to explain why. And I really didn't want to do that.

"Oh, God," Thurman moaned. "There isn't any good way out of this, is there?"

"What? No. No, there isn't. Darla Hayden has apparently been beaten to death in Aaron Hiller's office, and there is no good way out of it. Are you going to call the police or am I going to lean out the window and yell for Mark and his cameraman?"

"I'll call from my office. Please don't yell. That would only make things worse."

I watched him leave, resisting the urge to yell. At least yelling would have an immediate effect. Sometimes when I feel I can't make a situation better, I make it worse, just so I don't feel powerless.

And standing there alone, shut in the small office with

Darla Hayden's body, I felt as powerless as I ever have in my life.

I was standing because I didn't even want to sit on the sofa, a black leather job that I hadn't even noticed on my first visit, which rested against the atta-boy wall of photos and certificates.

Curtis walked through the office door a very long thirty seconds later, closing it again behind him.

"Oh, God," he said, looking at Darla. "Oh, God. I suppose we can't move her."

"No, we can't. Thurman already touched her to make certain she was dead. We can't touch her again."

"Are you all right?" He turned and held out his arm, offering shelter.

I looked into his serious brown eyes, and part of me wanted to accept.

"Not quite, but I can handle it."

I reached up and brushed his hand, pulling mine back before he could take it. He smiled briefly and nodded.

"Let me know if I can help," he said.

"Could you check to make sure that Thurman called the police?"

"I passed him in the hall. I promised the van had left." He shut his eyes, and I almost reached for his hand. "I hope Mark forgives the breach of faith."

"Come on. How can you mention faith and a TV news reporter in the same sentence?"

"My work as a consultant is based on the faith people have in me. Since Mark's employer hired me, I've worked to establish that faith in my relationship with him and with the others at the station. He will probably feel that I let him down by not telling him what was going on. A breach of faith. Especially since there's also faith involved in Mark's relationship with his career. He takes it seriously, even if it isn't one you'd choose."

I struggled with that one.

"You think he has a professional ethic?"

"Yes, I do. Brianne has one, as well. Just as you do." He looked at me again, and I resisted the urge to touch him.

"I'm not quite up for a discussion of the relativity of values right now," I said. "Can we save it for later?"

"For lunch." He offered another brief smile. "If we ever get it."

"The police are on the way." Thurman slid through the door, barely opening it. His face was still white, his eyes slightly unfocused, darting from me to Curtis, anywhere but Darla's body. "What now?"

"Now we wait in the hall," I said. "We've already trampled the carpet and touched the door, and you touched both the body and the window as well. We don't want to make a mistake and mess up anything more, even by accident."

"In the hall?" Thurman gasped. "People will see us, they may ask."

"Okay. I'll wait in the hall," I said. "You go back to your office and wait there."

"Randy, everybody's going to know about this," Curtis said gently. "It doesn't make any difference where we wait. Have you called Aaron? I'm sure he'd appreciate hearing from you before he hears from the police."

"Oh, God," Thurman moaned again. "You're right."

He slipped back out, pulling the door shut.

"I still think the hall is where we belong," I said.

"Okay."

Curtis held the door for me. I'd just as soon he didn't do that, but it wasn't the moment to protest.

We stood stiffly, barely over the threshold, silently. Having nothing to say with Curtis was a rare experience, and I didn't like it.

A student in denim shorts and a white tank top that exposed a little too much cleavage walked up to us.

"Is Dr. Hiller in?" she asked Curtis, brushing dark wisps of hair out of her face.

"No. He'll be here later. This isn't a good day to try to talk with him, though," he replied.

"But I need to see him—I have to get into his seminar, or I won't be able to graduate on time."

"Oh, for God's sake!" I snapped.

She turned, startled, as if she had just noticed me.

Curtis held up a hand to encourage me to keep quiet.

"I know that's important to you," he said. "And I'm sure Dr. Hiller will do what he can to help. Why don't you check with the department secretary to set up an appointment for another afternoon?"

She was all set to argue. The sight of Randy Thurman and two guys in dark blue uniforms barreling down the hall convinced her that maybe she shouldn't. She nodded and backed away in the other direction.

I had met one of the two cops before, and we exchanged short introductions all the way around. They had no problem when I suggested that Curtis and I might wait in the faculty center until someone wanted to talk with us.

When we resurfaced into the sunlight, the campus looked so normal that I felt a surge of anger. I was tempted to shout that Darla Hayden had been murdered. Tempted one more time to make things worse since I couldn't make them better. I resisted.

"Are you second-guessing the way you handled things Friday night?" Curtis asked.

"No. Sort of," I admitted.

"This isn't your failure. You didn't beat her up. You do know that."

"Hell, I didn't even bail her out," I said. "Although at some point I have to call the person who did."

I thought about Helen Stern. Darla Hayden would never resume therapy—she wouldn't even make her hearing on Tuesday—and if Helen Stern had acted in good faith, so had I. So, probably, had Darla.

We walked down the concrete ramp toward the same glass doors we had used to enter the Friday night gathering. And even second-guessing, I couldn't come up with a better way of dealing with the situation. The only bad guy here was the one who had murdered her.

I managed to open the door for myself.

The round tables that had been whisked away for the cocktail party were back in their usual positions. We were late enough that most of the lunch crowd was gone. We took a table near the door, one with a view of Manzanita Lake and the heavy growth of surrounding shrubs that gave the pond its name.

"Hi, what'll you have?"

The voice was so perky that I froze.

"Start with two cups of coffee and give us a moment," Curtis said.

"Sure thing, Dr. Breckinridge."

"How do you do it?" I asked.

"Do what?" His eyebrows rippled upward.

"Put other people's needs before your own. Whoever is around, you deal with that person first. Then yourself."

The eyebrows settled down again.

"No. That's not quite right. I've simply discovered that the best way of meeting my own needs is through other people. And it's easiest to do that when they aren't anxious about themselves."

I didn't think I had a chuckle in me, but one emerged anyway.

"Jesus, Curtis, you are smart."

"Yes, I know."

We were both chuckling when the student delivered the two cups of coffee. I had to stop chuckling before it got out of control and I cried.

"Need a little more time?" the student asked.

"Yes, thank you," Curtis said.

"I don't mean to rush you, Dr. Breckinridge, but the kitchen closes in about fifteen minutes." The student frowned as if Curtis held his future in his hands. The power of the faculty.

"I'm not sure I can do it," I said.

"How about soup?" Curtis asked.

"Are you serious?"

"Absolutely. Monday soup is cream of broccoli, and

French onion is available daily. I recommend the cream of broccoli."

"We're out," the student said. "But if you order the French onion, I'll get you some garlic bread at no charge."

"Okay." I got it out somewhere between a chuckle and a sob. The world was not coming to an end because the faculty center was out of broccoli soup.

"Make it two," Curtis told him.

"I thought only mothers recommended soup," I said after the student had dashed off.

"Soup is one of the things mothers are right about. You don't need to think about it, it makes you warm inside, and it's easy to digest. Any day, I expect a scientist to announce that chicken soup stimulates the production of endorphins." He smiled, and I managed a smile in return.

"All the runners and the chocolate eaters will be annoyed with the discovery," I said.

"Yes, but the mothers of the world will be vindicated."

We were still smiling at each other when the student returned with the soup and the garlic bread.

French onion soup actually does require attention, because the little strands of onion slip off the spoon, and the melted cheese on top sticks together when you try to cut through it. But I hadn't had anything except coffee all day, and the soup did make me feel better.

The sense of well being shriveled away when I saw Detective Matthews coming down the walk toward the doors, gray hair mussed, tie loosened, open jacket exposing the beer belly that hung over his khakis.

He slid into the chair between us.

"You look terrific, O'Neal. What's going on?"

I had forgotten about the television makeup.

"I fell into the hands of a mad cosmetician," I said. "And I didn't know my next stop would be watching over a dead body."

"Tell me," he said, nodding.

"I wish I could. Detective Matthews, Professor Breckinridge."

They looked each other in the eye and shook hands in that weird not-quite-arm-wrestling way guys use when they're testing each other. I could almost see their chests puff.

"You knew the deceased?" Matthews asked.

"I knew who she was," Curtis answered.

"Yeah. And you were here when she was picked up on a misdemeanor Friday night." Matthews paused to let both of us nod. "The fella whose office it was. He boffing her?"

Curtis winced.

"Used to," I said. "Probably not for a while."

"I understand he's on his way to campus. I hope he shows up."

"No," Curtis said. "You can't consider him a suspect. I know you have to check him out, since she was found in his office, but Aaron wouldn't have done it."

Matthews shrugged his shoulders as if he wasn't interested in Curtis's opinion. "We'll talk to him anyway."

"Of course. But you can't seriously think that Aaron Hiller would murder someone." Curtis was measuring his words carefully.

"Why not?" Matthews leaned forward. His weight rocked the small table.

"Aaron Hiller is a thoughtful man," Curtis said. "An intelligent man. I saw the body. Whoever beat that woman wasn't rational."

"Yeah," Matthews said. "I agree with that last part. You got any other suspects in mind?"

Curtis looked down at the table. "I don't suppose it could be an act of random violence."

"Possible. Not likely," Matthews said.

"You're not going to be happy about this," I added. "The odds are that the murderer is not only someone Darla knew, but someone you know, too."

"I'll have to take some time with that," Curtis said.

"Okay." Matthews turned to me. "I hear you were hired to find her. Who?"

"A collection agency."

"What kind of help can you give me with friends or relatives?"

"None of either in Reno, as far as I know. Just the therapist who bailed her out of jail."

Matthews nodded. "Tell me about this therapist."

"Nice woman. Caring. And yeah, I'll break the news to her."

Matthews nodded again. He lifted himself out of the chair. "Thanks, O'Neal. I gotta get back, see if anybody's heard from Hiller. Check in after you talk to the therapist, will you?"

"Sure. See you."

Curtis didn't bother to acknowledge Matthews' departure. He kept staring at the table.

"I have to go see Helen Stern," I said. "Are you okay?"

"I think it's all just starting to hit me," he answered.

"Yeah, I know." I thought about taking his hand, the one that was balled into a fist. "The adrenaline from the crisis is wearing off, and you're beginning to realize what it all means. Come on, I'll drop you off at your place. The soup helped me. I bet a nap would help you."

"What about my car?"

"I suspect you're upset enough to be a danger to yourself and others. And your car ought to be safe enough in the faculty lot for one night."

He nodded.

"Anything else?" The student waiter was suddenly at our table, waving a check.

"No. Do you have a pen?"

"Sure." The student put the bill on the table and handed Curtis a ballpoint pen.

Curtis scribbled his name and dropped the pen.

"Let's go." I held out my hand, because I wasn't certain he could get up without it. He uncurled the fist and reached out.

"Are you okay, Dr. Breckinridge?" the student asked.

"Just a little faint," he answered. "Nothing to worry about." He tried to fake a smile.

I got him out the door and up the walk. His hand was clammy, and I hoped he wasn't going into shock.

"You think I'm an idiot, don't you?" he asked.

"No. I think you're proving that your apparent attachment to the people around you is real. You really care that somebody got murdered. And the idea that a colleague might be a murderer really bothers you. I don't think you're an idiot at all. I might even describe you as admirable." I discovered I had been squeezing his hand when he squeezed mine in return.

"Thanks."

The area east of the student union was dotted with ragged groups, mostly students, some faculty and staff, all focused on the two black-and-whites and the un-marked blue Plymouth parked illegally in front of the business administration building. The Channel 12 news van was just pulling up behind them.

"Anybody you want to talk to?" I asked.

"Not now." Curtis sighed and shook his head. "Not right now."

We crossed behind the gym to the parking lot. The quarters I had dropped in the meter hadn't bought quite enough time. I stuck the ticket in my pocket.

Curtis slumped into the passenger seat of the Jeep. I pulled out of the lot and headed south on Virginia Street.

There aren't a lot of high-rise apartment buildings in Reno—growth has tended to sprawl outward rather than soar up, except for maybe a dozen major hotels. The cluster of buildings on Arlington, south of Wingfield Park, was a rare exception.

Curtis lived in one of them. I knew which because I had picked him up and dropped him off before, although I had never gone inside.

"I could come back after I've talked to Helen Stern," I said as we crossed the Truckee River. "If you want me to."

"I'd like that very much."

I made a U-turn in order to leave Curtis at the door of his building, which left me pointed in the wrong direction. I drove Island to Rainbow to Court and was only a couple of blocks from Helen Stern's office.

This time there was no note on the door. I pushed the doorbell.

The old, grated peephole flipped open. I could see one shadowed eye and part of a cheek.

"I took care of it," she said. "You're officially off the case."

"It isn't that. I have to talk with you."

"Go ahead."

I was too tired to argue.

"Darla Hayden was murdered."

The peephole shut. A moment later the door opened. Helen Stern motioned me in.

"That better not be some kind of sick joke."

"Fuck you."

I was about four inches taller and looking straight down at her. She blinked, but didn't retaliate.

"In my office," was all she said.

I didn't sit. I needed to keep the height advantage. She leaned against the edge of her desk, crossing her arms as if she needed to be hugged, and there was no one but herself available to do it.

"Randolph Thurman found the body a couple of hours ago. In Aaron Hiller's office. I don't know anything more."

"That bastard. That foul bastard."

She rocked forward so far that I thought she might fall, but she caught herself and rocked back again.

"The police are going to question both men, but it may be a few days before they even know for certain how she died. They'll take even longer to figure out who did it."

She froze, staring straight at me. "You mean Aaron Hiller is such a public figure that nobody wants to arrest him for something as sordid as beating a doctoral student to death."

"What makes you think she was beaten?"

"Wasn't she?" When I didn't answer, Helen Stern continued. "You don't think this was the first time, do you?"

"Shit." I had to sit down after all. "Did she ever report it?"

"No. I tried to convince her that she should, but she wouldn't. She was too humiliated, too ashamed that she had tolerated the abuse for as long as she did." Helen Stern rocked again, low and upright.

"She made the emotional abuse public. Why not the physical abuse?"

"What she made public she saw as professional abuse, an abuse of power and privilege. Her feelings were complicated, and I'm not sure I can simplify them for you."

"I'm not sure that you should." I realized that I had crossed my arms, too, almost hugging myself, and I worked to uncross them. "Whatever she told you confidentially in life is still confidential in death. And an unconfirmed report of prior physical abuse wouldn't be accepted in court under any circumstances."

"No. Well. I suppose we just have to wait and see what happens next, don't we?"

"Yes. We do." I forced myself to stand.

"Thank you for coming," she said. "I understand that telling me wasn't easy for you, and you did it because you thought I should hear about Darla from you before I heard from the police. I'm grateful for that. And I hope we meet again under better circumstances."

I was on my way out the front door when she called, "If that makeup is for a man, I hope he appreciates you."

I closed the door behind me.

If Curtis behind the wheel of a car would have been a danger to himself and others, the same charge could be leveled at me. I walked the couple of blocks down Court to Arlington and cut over to his building.

I rode the elevator to the seventh floor. The hall looked like a hotel corridor. A small hotel. There were only eight doors.

I pushed the buzzer on 702.

Curtis took so long to answer that I almost rang again. He opened the door dressed in a blue flannel bathrobe.

"I'm sorry I kept you waiting, but I took your advice about the nap. Come on in, and I'll put some clothes on."

"I don't have to stay," I said.

"How about a cup of tea?"

"Okay. Thanks."

I entered into a room unlike any man's living quarters I had ever experienced. Not just because it was clean and uncluttered—white sofa pillows fluffed, books on the shelves, copper-potted plants flourishing in their nooks—but because the inhabitant was so obviously someone who paid attention to his environment. One more way in which Curtis walked his talk.

The efficiency kitchen was only a low counter away. He filled two pottery mugs from a five-gallon spring water dispenser and stuck them in the microwave.

"Herbal or Earl Grey?" he asked.

"Whatever you're having. I like the Rauschenberg."

A huge lithograph took up the entire wall over a low tiled fireplace.

"Thanks. I'm having lemon grass."

"Fine."

When the microwave dinged, he stuck bags in the mugs and brought them to the glass-topped coffee table.

"How did the therapist take the news?" he asked.

"Not well."

"What else?"

"Oh, hell." I moved over to the sofa and sat down beside him. "She said Aaron had beaten Darla before."

"Oh, hell," he echoed. "What are you going to do?"

"Nothing. It's not my job."

"No."

We sat while the tea steeped.

"Do you mind if I turn on the news?" he asked.

"Go ahead."

Channel 12 had broken into regular programming to present a live report from the campus. Mark Martin was speaking earnestly to the camera.

". . . refused to make a statement. However, this reporter heard that he has agreed to talk to police tomorrow morning with an attorney present."

The next shot was the newsroom set. Lane Josten was smiling inappropriately at the camera, as if he didn't know they were covering anything more serious than the weather. Brianne McKinley looked pale but composed.

"Mark, what's the mood on campus?" she asked.

"Shock and anger, both at the murder of a doctoral student and at the possibility that a well-known professor may be responsible." His cowlick had popped up. He had to be aware how hard it was to take seriously the opinion of a young man with an unruly cowlick.

"If Professor Hiller hasn't even been charged, we can't rush to conclusions here," Brianne said firmly.

"Of course, you're right, Brianne," Mark said. His pictures was cut in next to hers in a split-screen shot. "But as far as we know, there are no other suspects at this time."

"Still, the death of Darla Hayden may be more complex than it seems at first glance." The camera moved in for a close-up of Brianne. Her eyes seemed to focus right at me. "Only this morning, I talked with a local private investigator and asked whether she had been hired to locate Darla Hayden."

A quick cut to a close-up of me, shifting uncomfortably in my chair, sweating through the makeup as if I had just auditioned for a Las Vegas chorus line.

"Well, yeah," the raccoon-eyed image of me said.

"Has Freddie O'Neal been on campus, Mark?" Brianne said when the camera had cut back.

"Yes, Brianne. She was here when the body was found."

A shot taken at the quad was cut in, showing me standing next to Curtis under a tree, listening to the student's speech.

"What the hell kind of professional ethic is this?" I muttered.

"You know what they're doing," Curtis said. "We can talk about it in a moment."

"We're certain the police are going to want to question both Miss O'Neal and whoever hired her," Brianne said. "I hope there are enough attorneys to go around."

Lane chuckled. "Right, Brianne. And Channel 12 will be with the story, all the way. We're going to take a break right now, but we'll be back in a moment with more live coverage of the Darla Hayden murder."

"This sucks," I said. "And I don't just mean the woman trying to sell me toothpaste that her father the dentist recommends."

I grabbed the remote from the coffee table and zapped the screen.

"You can turn it back on when I'm gone." I started to get up from the couch, but I had somehow gotten entangled with Curtis's arm.

"What would you do if you were Brianne and you didn't want the court of public opinion to judge Aaron before he had a chance to offer a defense?" he asked.

"If I were a television news anchor, I'd stay away from the story. News people are supposed to be objective observers. She's actually part of the story herself. Which she didn't mention. If I were romantically involved with Aaron Hiller and I had a public forum—which I think is what you were asking—I'd want to point out that there might be other suspects." I tried without a lot of success to keep my voice under control. "But she knew I was hired by a collection agency. She intentionally misled the viewers by pretending to be objective and then not telling everything she knew."

"I doubt that she sees it that way. You've met the therapist, for example. She hasn't."

"Come on. You don't suspect Helen Stern."

Serious brown eyes gazed into mine. "I don't want to suspect Aaron Hiller. And right now, there's no hard evidence against him. Give me some choices."

"Shit." I pushed my empty tea mug away. "I ought to go talk to Matthews. I said I'd check in after I talked to Helen Stern."

"Is that what you want to do?"

"No. I'm too tired to move."

"How about a beer?"

"You have beer?"

"I meet other people's needs, remember?"

I disengaged myself from his arm.

"I'll have a beer anyway."

I watched him move to the kitchen and retrieve two bottles of beer from the refrigerator. If I had been the one in the bathrobe, I could never have moved that easily, that unself-consciously.

There's something basically sexy about bathrobes. I hadn't intended to say that out loud, but when Curtis handed me the beer, he leaned over and kissed the corner of my eye.

"I have another one, if you'd like to join me."

If I'd thought, I'd probably have said no.

"Where is it?"

I guess I decided not to think.

"In the bedroom closet. I'll get it."

I knew I was only going to be able to move once. I grabbed his hand and pulled myself up.

"Show me," I said.

# Chapter 7

THERE'S NOTHING EROTIC about death. Particularly murder. But there is something about it, especially when the fallen sparrow was a woman whose haunted eyes had met one's own just a few days before, something that creates a profound need for intimacy with another live human being. The alternative—when intimacy isn't available—is a terrifying isolation, a feeling that the woman who died may not be the only one frozen out of life.

Under the right circumstances, intimacy becomes sensuality becomes eroticism.

That Monday afternoon, the circumstances were excellent.

We got up around sunset and raided Curtis's refrigerator, behaving like a couple of teenagers on a holiday. He put together a makeshift dinner of French bread and cheese and raw vegetables with bottled dressing for a dip. By mutual consent we left the television off.

I wouldn't call it the Fourth of July. But it did remind me of Thanksgiving. When I left for home the next morning, I was grateful to whatever powers govern the universe that Curtis Breckinridge was part of my life.

Butch and Sundance were waiting on the front porch. Sundance stretched and dug his nails into the wood to let me know he was glad to see me. Butch hopped off the steps into the grass and turned his back.

"No guilt trips," I said. "Although I am sorry you're upset, and if you want to come in, I'll feed you."

Butch thwacked his tail a couple of times and stayed put. Sundance followed me to the door, cheerfully rubbing my leg.

The reason Butch wasn't hungry became clear when I almost stepped on the head and right wing of what must once have been a rather large robin, left strategically behind my desk. I had been drawn there by the blinking light on my answering machine.

The messages were from my mother, Sandra, and Matthews.

"Please just call me," Ramona said, "because I don't even know where to start. You would have looked wonderful on the news if you hadn't been so nervous. And I hope your friend Curtis isn't a suspect in the murder. The dead girl wasn't your client, or anything like that, was she? I'll be home all day Tuesday. Please call."

"Take a look at the morning paper," Sandra said. "Then give me a call at the office. I'm available for lunch."

"I'm still waiting, O'Neal. Call me," Matthews said.

I had glanced at the *Herald* before leaving Curtis's apartment. The murder was on the front page, and an editorial blasted Brianne McKinley for not disclosing her personal connection—left undefined—with Aaron Hiller.

So I called Sandra first.

"Noon at Harrah's," I said.

"See you then."

Sundance was losing his good humor, and I decided to open a can before returning more calls, and before a second robin joined the first on my office carpet. I had barely dumped the cat food in a dish when the phone rang. I set the dish on the kitchen floor and returned to my desk, carefully avoiding the remains of the bird.

"Hi. How are you?" Curtis asked.

"Fine. Really fine."

"Good. Me, too."

"Good."

"Uh, I was going to call you this afternoon, but then I remembered that my car was still at the university. So could you give me a ride back?"

"Sure. When do you need to be there?"

"Not till two. We could have lunch."

Shit.

"I'm busy for lunch. I can get you to the university before or after." I was going to stop there, but I couldn't. "I'm free for dinner."

"Great. So am I. Could you pick me up at eleven? I'll have lunch on campus, and we can make plans for dinner."

"Sure."

When I hung up the phone, I had an uncontrollable surge of euphoria. I picked up robin feathers until it subsided. Then I called Matthews.

"Sorry," I said. "I really did intend to get back to you yesterday. I talked to the shrink, and she hopes Hiller did it. Says he beat her up before. No evidence, though."

"Yeah. No offense if I send somebody to get an official statement." He didn't wait for a response. "And let me know if you hear anything from your boyfriend's buddies."

He hung up before I could bristle.

I thought about calling Ramona. But I wanted to make amends to Butch. And I needed to take a shower and get myself more or less together before picking up Curtis and having lunch with Sandra.

I went back to the front porch. Butch was watching the door, a gray puffball with amber eyes blazing. I squatted down to his level.

"You think I'm unfaithful, I know," I told him. I considered pointing out that he was a cat, but I knew it wouldn't help. "Look. I'm doing my best. Please come in and eat cat food."

He didn't budge. He just kept staring. So I picked him up and carried him in. His legs stuck out at angles, and he refused to curl up.

I was reminded uncomfortably of the way I had reacted when Ramona started seeing Al.

"I don't have a lot of time right now," I said, stroking his fur, "but I'll be home later."

Butch refused to relent. And when I showed him the dish of some goo labeled mixed grill, he kicked it over. One more thing to clean up.

By the time the robin was disposed of and the preferred alternative—mine, anyway—was in a right-side-up cat dish, I had to keep moving in order to shower, dress, and get back to Curtis's place by eleven.

Returning Ramona's call would have to wait.

Curtis was standing in front of the building when I pulled up.

I had always thought he was nice looking. I was startled to discover how handsome he had suddenly become.

Overnight, as it were.

He climbed into the Jeep and kissed me.

"Hi," he said.

"Hi."

"The truth is, I felt absolutely elated when I realized that my car was still on campus. I was sure you'd pick me up, and it meant I got to see you that much sooner."

I felt a rush of blood to my face, and I had to turn away.

I got very busy putting the car in gear and driving north on Arlington.

"About dinner tonight," I said. "I really need to let Deke know what's going on. Would you mind the coffee shop at the Mother Lode?"

"No. Not at all. I'll look forward to it."

Neither of us could manage more than small talk the rest of the way. I dropped him off near the brick pillars at the main entrance. He kissed me again.

"See you."

This time I had enough self-possession to kiss him back.

I turned left on Virginia, dropped down to Second, and took the alley entrance to Harrah's parking garage. I reached the coffee shop just early enough to lose one Keno ticket before Sandra arrived.

She slid onto the red vinyl banquette across from mine, dropping her heavy black bag in the corner.

"All right. How did you get involved in this?" she asked.

"That's one of the things I like about you, Sandra— your amazing capacity for small talk."

"What is it you don't want to tell me?"

She clasped her hands and leaned forward, smiling her professional smile. For a moment, Sandra reminded me of Brianne McKinley. Sculpted blond hair, carefully applied makeup, an ivory blouse and light-blue jacket that would have warmed the senses of her viewers. And Sandra had been on television.

"Brianne has your old job, doesn't she?" I countered. "Do you envy her?"

She blinked, and I regretted the question.

"No. Really, no. I did a little, at the beginning, when I saw her sitting in my chair, on my set. I missed the ego stroke that comes from working in front of a camera every day—an ego stroke that I wasn't even aware of until it was gone. For about a year I was hard on Don and a little angry with the baby, and I'm sorry about that now. I had to take time, had to learn to express myself by writing, not by talking. It wasn't easy." She took a deep breath, and then rewarded me with a personal smile. "But now that I'm across the river, I'm glad I plunged in. I have a freedom as a journalist that I didn't have as a TV news reader. That's what I was, what Brianne is, no matter what the station says. Working for the *Herald*, I can write my own copy. All I have to do is label what I write as opinion, and I can say whatever I want. A few people get to do that on television, but not many. Brianne injected an opinion into last night's newscast— unlabelled—and I think it's going to cost her. So I don't envy her, although she probably wouldn't believe me."

"Okay. I do."

"Want to replay that ticket?" The Keno runner had appeared next to the table.

"Not right now," I said.

"That's a first." Sandra arched her eyebrows.

"Yeah, well, there's a lot going on."

"Ready to talk yet?"

"Where's the waitress?"

I caught the attention of a young woman in a black miniskirt and a white ruffled apron. She took our order—two chicken salads—and left. Sandra was still watching me.

"This all has to be off the record," I said.

"Come on. I don't betray a trust. Tell me what I can use, what I can't."

"Oh, hell. Darla Hayden dropped out of sight, her shrink turned the bill over to a collection agency, she turned up at the faculty party with a toy gun, then she turned up dead in Aaron Hiller's office. That's public."

Sandra nodded. "As is her affair with Aaron Hiller."

"The shrink says he used to beat her up. That's not public."

"Great. We got him."

"Shit." I shook my head. "Curtis doesn't think he

could do it. Curtis knows him, and Curtis doesn't like him much. He still doesn't think he could do it."

"Curtis?" Sandra said it gently, as if she didn't want me to think she was prodding.

"Yeah." I did my best not to blush. "And I respect his opinion."

"I'm really pleased to hear that. I hope it works out. Whatever it is," she added quickly.

"Thanks. You know anything I don't?"

"Well, Curtis may know, and he may have told you. Horton Robb is devastated, because he is almost as fond of Brianne as he is of ratings, but he asked her to take tonight off, and he may have to ask her to take an extended vacation."

"Do you think she'll lose her job?"

Sandra shook her head. "Too soon to tell. Horton said Steve Burns is pressuring him to look for a replacement, but Horton is hoping he can ride out the storm. Keep Brianne, and keep her off this particular story, since she's part of it."

"Is she even aware that she violated a journalistic taboo?"

"Of course she is. She isn't stupid. Horton thinks she's betting that her involvement will translate into even higher ratings. Horton is in many ways an old-school gentleman, though, and if it becomes a real circus, he'll let her go."

I shook my head in harmony. "Aaron Hiller isn't worth it."

"You don't like him."

"I don't really know him. In person, he struck me as a

charming phony. Brianne McKinley struck me the same way. In Darla's memos and Helen Stern's comments— she's the shrink—Hiller's a real bastard."

"Memos?" Sandra's eyebrows arched again.

"She circulated some memos to the faculty, charging unfair treatment in her exams, among other things. I'm not sure they ought to be published."

"Would Darla Hayden have wanted them published?"

"Absolutely. But campus administrators would have another opinion." I paused, appreciating the rapt attention Sandra was giving me. "I'll give you a copy on condition we discuss in advance anything you want to print."

"Done."

The waitress deposited our salads, and Sandra barely missed a beat.

"Are there any suspects besides Hiller?" she asked.

"I don't think so. Not at this point, anyway. Which doesn't mean there won't be, once Matthews starts a real investigation."

"What's bothering you? Curtis?"

"Yeah, a little. More than that, though, is the fact that Hiller is smart. Even his detractors think he's brilliant. Why would a smart guy kill his ex-girlfriend in his office and leave her there?"

"Well, if he's smart enough, he might do it to argue that he's too smart to do it. Argue that it has to be a frame."

"Maybe."

"Curtis is definitely having an effect on you."

"What?"

"You're eating the fruit first."

I looked down at my plate. The chicken salad had been garnished with slices of pineapple and watermelon and a couple of underripe strawberries. And Sandra was right. I had started with the fruit.

"I like fruit."

"And you used to treat it as dessert. Now you're going for it. I was wondering if the makeup was another change when I saw the news last night."

"What? You have to be kidding."

She gestured until she swallowed. "Why? You looked terrific. Is a clean face a political statement? Is it a professional advantage to blend with the wallpaper? Do you have something against looking attractive? Tell me."

"I don't know what to say." I wanted to tell her I was annoyed at the questions. "I looked at myself in the mirror, when the makeup guy was through, and the woman with the eyes wasn't me. I'm not sure it's any more complicated than that."

"Well, think about it. Maybe you could try being her for special occasions."

"Why?" The word erupted, and I lowered my voice. "God, you sound like my mother. Who I am isn't good enough. I ought to be somebody else."

Sandra reached over and grabbed my wrist. "I'm sorry. That isn't it. Who you are is better than good enough, and you know I believe that. You also know I believe in establishing an image as a personal choice. I can accept that we chose different images. I'm sorry. Please."

"I'm sorry. I didn't mean to yell. It's you on top of my mother on top of Curtis seeing me as more attractive with makeup, and I don't know what I want to do about it."

"Well, you don't have to decide this minute. See how it goes with Curtis, see what you want to do." She released my wrist.

"Shit." I put my fork down and pushed the plate away.

"Giving up on the chicken salad won't help you decide."

Her forehead wrinkled, and I began to feel guilty.

"Curtis said it's his problem, not mine. I'm just not sure." I took another bite of the chicken.

"Well, it's a cultural problem, as long as you've decided to disown it."

"Or a species problem. If we were peafowl, Curtis would be obligated to put on a show."

"Absolutely. And even without the show, Curtis sounds fascinating. I can't wait to meet him. I'll have to check with Don, but why don't we think about having dinner Friday night?" She displayed the bright, professional smile again.

"I'll get back to you on that. I'm not sure I'm ready for a double date." In truth, I hadn't realized how many dinners were going to be spent introducing Curtis. And I didn't know whether it was a good idea to invest so much just yet.

"Well, let me know when you are."

"Okay. Moving back a step in the conversation, you've been talking as if you and Horton Robb are great friends. People aren't usually that close to a former boss."

"I know, but Horton insisted. At first I thought he was being friendly to keep me from suing when he didn't want to accommodate my pregnancy. I finally realized he simply likes me. His opinion that pregnant women don't belong on television was nothing personal." Sandra laughed.

I didn't think it was that funny.

"Why didn't you sue?"

"Lawsuits eat up your life, and I wanted to get on with mine. Besides, I told you, I didn't want the job back."

"That must have been a relief for Brianne. Did Horton tell you about her affair with Hiller?"

The waitress caught sight of my apparently abandoned plate and started in our direction. I was getting hungry again, so I picked up my fork and stabbed another hunk of chicken.

"No. Lane did. We were buddies when we worked together, and we still have lunch once every couple of months. He's such a sweetheart."

"Oh, hell." I sighed when the realization hit me.

"What?"

"I do need to get you together with Curtis. He ought to have whatever background you can give him on the Channel 12 cast of characters. Although if Brianne is fired, it may not matter."

"Horton told me he had hired Curtis as a consultant." Sandra's smile was almost a smirk. "I wasn't going to mention that—I was afraid it would come out too much like blackmail."

"No, it's okay. Friday. I'll ask him."

"Horton's impressed with his insight and intelligence," Sandra added.

"Okay. I'll ask him if he's free for dinner Friday."

I ate a few more bites of the chicken salad while Sandra finished hers. I had never been part of the world of couples. Curtis had. I wasn't certain how I was going to fit.

Sandra was facing a deadline on a story about the upcoming election for governor. She conceded that Darla Hayden's murder was going to siphon off interest, but she swallowed half a glass of iced tea and dashed off anyway.

I took Second Street toward home. I considered checking at the police station to see if Matthews knew anything more about the cause of death, but I decided that the evening news would tell me all I really needed to know, and I could wait a few hours.

Since there was no blinking light on my answering machine, and no cats on my desk, I didn't stop in my office. Reassuring Butch was a higher priority than calling Ramona.

I found both cats curled up on the bed, still unmade from Sunday night, when I had last slept in it. I moved Butch carefully onto my lap, so that he wouldn't wake up enough to remember he was mad at me.

The phone rang just as I had him settled and purring, and I considered letting the machine pick it up. I stretched out my arm and barely managed to grab the receiver without disturbing the cat.

"Good afternoon, Miss O'Neal. It's Aaron Hiller."

"What?"

Hiller's smooth, low voice was so unexpected that I was almost speechless.

"I'm calling from my attorney's office. He has urged me to plan for the possibility that I may be charged with a serious crime. We'd like to hire you to help with the defense. Are you available?"

"I'm not sure. I'd have to think about it."

"Think about it overnight. Then meet me here tomorrow morning at eleven."

In a burst of temporary insanity, I agreed.

# Chapter 8

"ARE YOU TELLING me this as a point of information or because you want my opinion?"

When I picked Curtis up for dinner, I started with the phone call even before his seat belt was buckled, because Aaron Hiller's request was still in the front of my head, vibrating like a strobe right behind my eyes. I hadn't expected a Socratic response.

"I suspect I know your opinion. You think he didn't do it, so you also think I ought to help keep him out of jail."

I was driving because I wanted the freedom to go home with Curtis or not. Watching his smooth, serious face as he pondered his answer, I was leaning toward yes. But if my anxiety level rose later on, I had the Jeep.

Inviting him to come home with me would have been a less attractive option. Curtis made better coffee than I did. Fortunately. He also had more interesting snacks in his refrigerator, although a trip to the supermarket would take care of that.

There was also Butch to consider. I didn't want him to freak out. If Curtis was going to be around for a while, we could work on Butch. If he wasn't, there was no point in making the cat nuts.

"Well, actually, no," Curtis said. "That isn't quite what I think. I hope Aaron didn't do it—which doesn't necessarily translate into hoping that you will become involved in what is certain to be a messy situation. And I'd never use language that would make your involvement a moral imperative—no 'ought.'"

"Okay. I give up. What's your opinion?"

His left hand rested gently on my shoulder.

"My opinion is that Aaron will need a good defense team. If he's charged with murder. I have no opinion yet on whether you should be part of it. That depends on what you want."

"I want whoever murdered Darla Hayden to fry in hell for it."

"Suppose you conducted an investigation and still had doubts about Aaron's innocence—could you work with his attorney to get him off?"

"Absolutely not."

Curtis shook his head. "Then say no. The American criminal court system is about advocacy. Justice is a jury's decision. If you disagree with that, don't participate."

I glared at him, but let it go long enough to pull into a parking space in the Mother Lode's high-rise garage. We crossed the alley to the casino, wound through the twisted aisle between the twenty-one tables, and rode the escalator to the coffee shop in silence.

Deke was waiting by the cashier's stand. I had left a

message on his answering machine, letting him know I was bringing Curtis with me, but I had somehow still expected him to be in his usual spot at the counter.

When I introduced them, the handshake stopped just short of an arm-wrestle. Even though Curtis and Deke were about the same height, Deke had a heavy weight advantage. I was relieved that he didn't push it.

I would have thought the macho posturing out of character for Curtis if he hadn't gotten into the same thing with Matthews. And actually, he had done it with Aaron Hiller in a more cerebral way. I'd have to remember not to underestimate how competitive he could be.

"I thought you might be more comfortable at a table," Deke said.

I envisioned an hour of sitting between the two of them at the counter.

"Thanks. But won't Diane feel slighted?"

Deke shook his head. "I already told her."

She was watching us from behind the counter. I waved, and she waved a coffeepot back.

"I'll take you over to meet her before we leave," I said to Curtis.

For a Tuesday evening in September, with tourist season winding down, the coffee shop was crowded. And the trouble with the few available tables would be the chance of possible eavesdroppers.

"Does anybody mind waiting for a booth?" I asked.

Neither of them did. We stood in silence, incapable of small talk, until one opened up in the far corner.

When I realized I was going to be stuck on the inside, I almost changed my mind. But I could stand a little claustrophobia for the sake of privacy.

"Aaron Hiller wants to hire me," I said as soon as we were settled.

"Good thing somebody does," Deke answered. "Otherwise, you'd have to keep out of it."

I winced, but he was right. "Yeah, I know. That's the upside—I can stay involved. On the downside, I'm not sure I should take his money when I think he may be guilty."

"You think," Deke emphasized. "You don't know. You find evidence that convinces you, you turn it over to Matthews, give back the money, and quit the case."

"That's one possibility," I said.

"Not a good one." Curtis's muscles had tensed. I could feel it where our thighs barely touched on the red vinyl banquette. "If the media picked it up—and they would— that would almost automatically deny Aaron a fair trial."

"A fair trial convicts the guilty and releases the innocent," Deke said, glowering.

"Yes. And, ideally, that's what happens. But however you feel about it, it's a jury's job to decide which is which."

"Okay." I didn't like having the conversation carried on without me. "What would you do with evidence that implicated Aaron in the murder?"

"I'd tell Aaron what I found—because he is a colleague—and then turn it over to Matthews. But I haven't been hired to help in his defense." Curtis said it calmly.

I patted his thigh to let him know I was aware of the tension under his words. I almost lost my train of thought by touching him.

"You're asking me to trust a jury," I said. "But trusting a jury is trusting the luck of the draw when you can't fold the hand. They aren't reliable. You know that. They can come up with all kinds of weird decisions. In California, they've even had hung juries after people confessed."

"And who are you, the pope? Your judgment is infallible?" Curtis picked up my hand and held it. "One of the earliest trials we have a record of—Orestes's trial for the murder of his mother, the original courtroom drama—was one in which the defendant confessed and the jury still couldn't reach a verdict."

I pulled my hand back. "The deciding vote, as I remember, was cast by Athena, the goddess who sprang from the head of Zeus dressed in full armor. She said she couldn't relate to having a mother, since she'd only had a father. Therefore, Orestes could go free. Not exactly relevant when we're talking about contemporary trials with ordinary people judging. And in high-profile cases, juries are asked to stop reading papers and watching television, so they're even less informed than ordinary."

"How about the jury that acquitted Lizzie Borden?" Deke asked.

"She didn't confess," I said.

"The maid might have done it," Curtis said almost at the same time.

"Ready to order?" The waitress was one I knew by sight, but this was my first time at her station.

She rounded the table quickly. A hamburger, a steak, and a grilled chicken breast with salad instead of fries. Three beers.

"I don't suppose you two want to go all the way back to Cain and Abel," Deke said.

"Actually, that makes my point," Curtis answered, leaning forward and resting his elbows on the table. He clasped his hands and rocked them slowly. "God didn't need a jury. But no single human being has the right to act as God."

"Let's stick with Orestes," I said. "What about the Furies? They judged him guilty."

"And the appellate court of Athenian citizens—with Athena presiding—reversed their decision," Curtis replied. He unclasped his hands and turned to include me. "It happens all the time. That's what appellate courts are for."

"But he was guilty, goddamn it. He killed his mother."

"Who had killed her husband, Orestes's father, who before that had sacrificed his daughter, Iphigenia, to the gods. It was a bloody family. Athena said the cycle of retribution had gone far enough." Curtis was starting to look exasperated.

Probably I was, too.

"You're saying that just because I disagree with a verdict here or a verdict there, I shouldn't take on the system. I'm not sure you're right." I made an effort not to raise my voice.

"He's partly right—you shouldn't take on the system—but that doesn't mean the system is right," Deke interjected.

"I'm saying you're smart, you're thoughtful, you're sincere, and you may be able to make the perfect decision as far as Aaron Hiller's guilt or innocence is concerned. But if you agree to work for his defense, and then subvert that defense, you are setting a precedent for people less smart and less sincere, just as surely as if you engaged in an act of overt vigilantism." Curtis had picked up my hand again. He gripped it in both of his.

I had to disentangle.

"Wow. I'll have to think about it."

"Do that," Deke said. "But don't lose no sleep over the cosmic ramifications of your decision."

"Not cosmic," Curtis snapped. "Just human."

"Now you're making my point," Deke snapped back. "Human ramifications. There be jurors voting to convict or acquit based on whose smile they like best, evidence be damned. If somebody is guilty—bare-assed, flat-out guilty—don't need more than one person to judge it."

"Like Singapore? Where people are coerced into confessing and then permanently scarred by the punishment? Where nobody appeals in case the next judge increases the sentence?" A knot appeared just above Curtis's jaw.

They were both taking this too personally.

I grabbed a Keno ticket and started marking numbers. I figured neither one would criticize me in case the other might defend the habit, and I was right. I pulled out a dollar and stuck the two pieces of paper under a salt shaker on the edge of the table. The runner smiled as she picked it up, the first time I had seen this particular runner smile.

The three of us were sitting in silence when the waitress brought our beers.

"Maybe you could talk a little more about Aaron Hiller," I said to Curtis once she had walked away and we had each taken a gulp. "Is there something more to your feeling that he's innocent? Or is it just that you know him?"

"Truthfully, it's just that I know him. That, and the fear that a rush to justice is going on. I'd like to see a search for other suspects."

Deke nodded. "That's a problem. Either of you know of other possibilities?"

Curtis and I both shook our heads.

"Darla Hayden doesn't seem to have had much of a life, except for her work," I said. "Neither her therapist nor her landlady saw her as a social butterfly."

"So if you agreed to help Aaron, where would you start?" Curtis asked.

"With other graduate students. Like the guy making the speech for the camera. And I'd talk to Hiller's wife."

"Jeannie?" Curtis set his beer down. "She's a less likely suspect than Aaron."

"Why?" I asked.

"For one thing, I don't think she's physically strong enough. For another, I can't imagine her taking that kind of action. She isn't stupid, but she is somehow mindless where Aaron is concerned. She adores him. She wouldn't put him in trouble."

"Then right now, my money's on her," Deke said.

"How well do you know her?" I asked.

"I've met her a few times at faculty functions. That's all. My opinion is based mostly on the stories of how they met coupled with her three-steps-behind body language when they come and go." Curtis took another sip of his beer.

Deke looked skeptical. I leapt in before he could turn it into another argument.

"You said she was his student, and he left his wife for her. Why couldn't she have been afraid that he'd do the same thing again?"

"A year ago, maybe. Not now. Aaron would never forgive the public embarrassment that Darla caused him."

"Hoomph," Deke said. "Back to Aaron."

"I still want to talk with her," I said.

The Keno numbers started lighting up. When both Deke and Curtis stopped to watch the numbers, I began to wish I hadn't played. When the blips stopped, and only two of my numbers showed, I quietly tore up the ticket.

The conversation through dinner moved in fits and jerks. Curtis and Deke couldn't find anything in common beyond an interest in whether Aaron Hiller would be charged with murder, and that was talked out by the time the waitress distributed the plates and brought a second round of beers.

I was relieved when the check appeared. Curtis reached for it, but Deke landed on it first.

"Thirds," I said, slipping it out from under Deke's paw.

Both of them nodded. Casino food is so cheap that nobody could make a big deal out of it.

The good-byes were as awkward as dinner. Diane was too busy to do more than wave when we stopped at the counter. Curtis and I left Deke at the foot of the escalator, and as we retraced our path between the tables, I almost wished I had handled the transportation differently. Deke had been my friend for a long time—outlasting any more intimate relationship with a man—and who knew what was going to happen with Curtis.

I would have to have dinner alone with Deke the next night and talk it out. Or whatever would pass for talking it out.

"I'm sorry it wasn't friendlier," Curtis said when we reached the Jeep.

"That's okay," I answered. "You haven't asked me to keep quiet around your friends. I'd expect you to speak your mind around mine. And another friend—Sandra Herrick—wants to know if you're free for dinner on Friday. That one ought to go a little better. She was Brianne's predecessor on the Channel 12 news. And I think she believes in the jury system. Not that it's perfect, just that it's better than the alternatives. Even if Singapore isn't the only other choice."

"That may have sounded like a straw man. But Singapore does illustrate the argument. Judges are not necessarily more trustworthy than juries. Police states achieve low crime rates at a terrible cost. And I am free for dinner Friday." His hand returned to my shoulder, where it had rested on the ride to the casino.

I hadn't realized I'd been holding my breath until I released it, and the tension started to drain. As I thought about it, Sandra would have been the better person to start with. There was no way Deke and Curtis would hit it off, or not without a lot of goodwill on both sides. If necessary, I would ask them both to evoke it. Curtis and Sandra at least had a few common interests.

"Do you want to come in?" he asked when we had crossed the Truckee and I had slowed the car.

"Well, really, yes. But I need to decide what to do about Aaron Hiller. And if I come in, the decision has to be to take the case."

"Why?"

"Because I can't think without talking about it, and I don't want to argue anymore."

"That makes sense." He nodded. I could just see the silhouette of his face in the glow from the streetlight. From the unusually round line of his cheek, I knew he was smiling. "Moment of truth, then. Do you want to come in?"

"Oh, hell. Do you promise to get me out of here in the morning early enough so that I can go home and change before meeting Aaron and his attorney?"

"Solemnly. I promise to make coffee first. Breakfast if you want it." The last two sentences were whispered in my ear.

"You're on."

I found a parking place half a block north. We walked back to the building and rode up in the elevator holding hands.

What scared me was how easily I could start to like being part of a couple. With all the questions that raised, with all the tensions that would have to be worked out—not just Deke, not just Butch, but life questions—I could still imagine being part of a couple.

The idea scared me so much that I excused myself as soon as we got inside Curtis's apartment. I leaned against the bathroom wall, taking deep breaths, until I calmed down. Letting my fears take over—whether it was the fear that getting involved meant someone else would try to run my life or the fear I'd want to stay and he'd want to leave, either one—wouldn't do me any good. If I got scared enough, I'd just end up bolting, and being stuck home alone with the cats one more time.

His bathroom was clean, white tile with a gray diamond pattern, navy-blue towels folded in thirds. I splashed cold water on my face, dried it, and carefully refolded the hand towel. I folded mine in halves, when I remembered to fold them. At least we both squeezed the toothpaste from the bottom.

When I returned to the living room, Curtis was seated on the white sofa. Two mugs of tea were waiting on the glass-topped coffee table.

"You okay?" His face had softened with concern.

"Yeah. I just have to ask one thing. Are you going to push me to start wearing makeup?"

"Only after you've gotten used to the fishnet stockings, the black satin corset, and the handcuffs. Is that what's bothering you?"

I sat down next to him. He put his arm out and pulled me close.

"I just don't know what the rules are," I said.

"There aren't any. We make it up as we go along."

"You mean I have to bet without seeing the cards?"

He nodded solemnly. "The luck of the draw."

I had to laugh. "Yeah. And here my game was always Keno."

"Time for a change." He kissed me on the corner of the mouth.

"Maybe." I kissed him back.

The segue from the couch to the bed was smoother than I expected. We carried the tea mugs with us and undressed together.

I had discovered the night before that Curtis had meant it when he said that the best way to get his own needs met was to first reduce the other person's anxiety. He still meant it.

Later, when the lights were out, and we were lying wrapped together like a classic sculpture, I started thinking again about the rest of my life. I remembered my question about makeup.

I asked it again.

Curtis kissed me on the forehead.

"You're an amazing woman, with makeup or without. I don't care what you decide. I love you either way."

"I think I'm starting to love you, too."

He kissed me again. "I know. Get some sleep."

I was too comfortable to bristle. I was just getting used to the curve of his shoulder and the light, musky smell of his body. And I wanted to sleep.

Curtis kept his promise in the morning, bringing me coffee before I was quite awake.

I turned down breakfast. I can't face breakfast first thing in the morning, and I really needed to move, to start the circulation in my limbs.

In truth, the fear was rising again. I needed to get out of there and reestablish my autonomy.

I left the Jeep parked on Arlington and jogged home.

Since I would be walking to the appointment with Aaron Hiller and his attorney, Roger Wade, I had to hurry. That meant ignoring the blinking light on the answering machine, refilling the cat food dish, and telling Butch that I would spend time with him later.

He was sitting in the hall, hunched and glaring, when I got out of the shower. I hugged him and dropped him on the bed, but it wasn't enough.

Sundance curled up happily on my discarded shirt, but Butch glared.

"Later. I'm sorry," I told him.

He still glared.

I trotted out the door and back downtown, to the bank building on First Street that held the offices of Steglich, Burkham, and Wade, attorneys-at-law.

The elevator took me to the top floor and opened onto a reception area tiled with burgundy and pink faux marble. A young woman wearing a headset checked to make certain I was expected. She was perched on a stool behind a high desk that looked straight out of *Star Trek*.

"Go to the end, turn left, first door on the right." She pointed down the hall and immediately returned to the flashing lights on the console.

Roger Wade met me at the corner. He was well over

six feet tall, with a square jaw and the kind of black wavy hair that would have become unruly if it had been a quarter of an inch longer. He and Lane Josten might have had the same barber.

He introduced himself and held out his hand.

"Basketball," I said as I shook it, tilting my face to inspect his. When you're as tall as I am, looking up as you shake hands is a rare experience. And a bit unnerving. "You were on the UNR team—the best one they ever had—but you graduated the year before I came. I'd almost forgotten."

"So has everyone else." The tight smile told me he wished somebody remembered. He ushered me through an open door.

Aaron Hiller was standing on the far side of the room, next to a long window that showed only the bubbling neon sign of the new casino across the street. Years earlier, before the city had become overgrown, there must have been a view of the mountains.

"I'm glad to see you, Miss O'Neal. I hope this means you've decided to help."

"Might as well start calling me Freddie, Aaron."

"Good." He laughed sharply, showing his teeth. "Have a seat, Freddie."

The office had two sides, a work area dominated by a mammoth teak desk and credenza and a schmooze area consisting of a black leather couch, two black leather recliners, and a low table. I took one of the recliners and Roger Wade took the other. Aaron had the couch to himself.

"I'd like to start with a couple of questions." I looked from one to the other, both men wearing dark suits carefully tailored to fit well-developed biceps and pecs. The Old Testament prophet and the Roman gladiator. I wondered if they had met in the weight room at the gym.

Roger glanced at Aaron, who nodded.

"What makes you think the police are going to charge you with Darla Hayden's murder?" I asked.

"Motive and opportunity." Aaron leaned toward me, offering his intimate smile. "She had been stalking me, she had publicly threatened me, and I agreed to talk with her that night in my office. I lost my temper and left. She was still alive and well. I have no idea who came in later, who killed her. But the district attorney may decide that the circumstantial case against me is strong enough to proceed."

"You left her in your office?"

"No. I left her in front of the building. I don't know how she got back in."

"Did she have a key?"

"I gave her one when we were working together. She had given it back long before. And I haven't given anyone else a copy."

"Okay. You said she'd been stalking you. I didn't know that."

Aaron blinked, but didn't lose his smile. "I didn't report it. My wife was the only one aware of it until last Friday night. I told Randy Thurman then. And the police officer, the woman."

"Okay." I wasn't happy about that. Somebody—like

Helen Stern—should have known. "Stalking you how? What did she do?"

"Mostly E-mail messages. They were from a student account, but I knew they were from her. I didn't keep a record. But I do have copies of memos—printed-out memos—that she distributed to the entire faculty on which she had scribbled postscripts for me. And she mailed a birthday card to the house."

"Yeah. Stalkers like to send birthday cards." When he didn't react, I added, "So what do you want from me?"

"We want you to come up with at least one other suspect, with enough evidence to cast reasonable doubt on the prosecutor's case." Roger answered that question. He didn't bother to smile. "That's all. Nobody's expecting you to produce the killer."

"Right. Last question. Why me?"

Roger deferred to Aaron again.

"A combination of your reputation and my own observation led me to conclude that you are both competent and intelligent. Besides, you've already done some leg work, met some of the people involved. If we hired someone else, we'd have to pay for that to be done all over again." The smile turned rueful. "Defending a criminal charge is expensive, Freddie, and I don't want to pay more than I have to."

That made sense. I still had an uneasy feeling that I was being co-opted. Hiller might be worrying about money, but he was also buying off a potential enemy.

"You do understand that I'll need to talk with both Brianne McKinley and your wife, Jeannie, don't you?" I had another question after all.

Aaron sighed and nodded, then flashed the rueful smile again. "Actually, that's one more reason for hiring you. I'd rather have them questioned by another woman. Although obviously, my first choice is that neither one be implicated."

That last sentence was a hurried afterthought. He didn't give a damn who was implicated as long as he was off the hook. Working for someone I didn't like might raise more problems than the philosophical ones about guilt and innocence.

"When do you want me to start?"

"As soon as you can," Roger said.

We discussed gritty stuff like bills and payment, exchanged phone numbers all around, including Brianne's unlisted one, and I left as soon as I reasonably could.

The day was overcast, and First Street seemed to get dingier every year. I walked past the old Methodist church, with its once-proud Gothic spires, huddled between two characterless professional buildings. The crumbling stones of the church were a sad reminder that this had once been a residential neighborhood in a pioneer town. Pioneer towns always had big churches. The early settlers had seemed to understand the need for balance, church and saloon, a balance between spiritual and material—even Apollonian and Dionysian—that had been tossed out around the time the railroad drove the stagecoach lines out of business.

The rise of commercial interests had signaled the ascendance of another set of values. Commerce was the worst of both worlds, an amoral, joyless approach to life based on keeping score. Doing the job not because it was right, or even exciting, but only because it paid.

I fantasized finding evidence to prove Aaron's guilt, refusing the money, and testifying against him. Maybe he would plea-bargain, and a fair trial wouldn't be an issue. Curtis would understand.

The Truckee was brown and sluggish, the tennis courts were empty, and I didn't stop in the park. I had to pass Curtis's apartment house on the way to pick up the Jeep, and I considered ringing his buzzer, but I wanted to get home. I needed a little time alone to sort out both the professional and the personal situation. They were churning together in my stomach, and I had to move at least one to my head. I could call him later and tell him what happened.

I doglegged across Virginia to Wheeler, wishing I felt more certain, more secure, more something, about my life. As I turned onto High Street, I spotted my mother's burgundy Oldsmobile parked in front of my house. I was reminded by a surge of guilt that I hadn't called her back in days. I would have headed in another direction, if I'd had another place to go.

Ramona was sitting on the porch step, wrapped in a quilted purple jacket that was too heavy for the light autumn chill. Her head was down, copper curls tumbling around her shoulders.

"Hi." I almost asked why she hadn't called to let me know she was coming. I remembered the blinking light on my answering machine in time.

She looked up, startled. Her eyes were red and her face puffy, as if she had cried until she was spent.

Sundance hopped out of her arms and shook himself, then stretched. I wondered how long Ramona had been there, and the surge of guilt turned to a flood.

"Al had a heart attack last night," she said. "He's in intensive care at St. Mary's, and I'm too exhausted to drive home. Please. I need to stay with you. Please."

Her face twisted, and she started to whimper like a child.

I sat down on the step and held her in my arms.

# Chapter 9

FROM THE AIR, it's hard to figure out why Reno became established exactly where it is. Verdi—a collection of scattered buildings about ten miles west, where the Sierras start to flex their muscles—appears to have been the logical choice for a burgeoning town. The spot where people who couldn't make it any further in the Conestoga would have hammered in the stakes. The banks of the Truckee River may be a little steeper there, but it isn't too steep or too swift to ford. Nevertheless, if you're traveling Interstate 80 west today and you blink, you'll miss Verdi. Even in the Cherokee, I only recognize the scattered buildings as Verdi because I know it's there.

The railroad station was built in Sparks, in theory three miles east of Reno, although in fact the border between Sparks and Reno was swallowed by motels long ago. But the city didn't grow up around the railroad station. It grew up around the casinos, a Big Bang spiraling out from the inn at Lake's Crossing, the original bridge across the Truckee River. Reno's existence was thus, to me, as illogical and imponderable as that of the universe.

Reno's internal geography, in contrast, had the or-
thogonal regularity of a Mondrian painting, divided in
quarters by Interstates 80 and 395, with small squares of
red and green and brown broken only by the meanders of
the Truckee, and the pop-up cartoons of Bally's and the
MGM Grand to the south.

I came to that conclusion on one specific Wednesday,
just before sunset, as I was taking the Cherokee in a wide
circle several hundred feet above Reno, the Biggest Little
City that has no reason to be where it is.

I was in a small airplane because I needed to be alone.

I had shifted mental gears from my own problems to
pondering Reno's existence because that was easier than
trying to figure out what I was doing with my life and
what crime I had committed to deserve the punishment
visited upon me, namely that my mother had just moved
in with me for an indefinite period.

Shit.

I had to let her stay.

The thought that my mother needed me was so
terrifying that I couldn't think about it and keep the plane
level at the same time. My hands would get sweaty on the
yoke, and the nose would start to rise. I would consciously have to relax my grip and push back until I could
spot the horizon.

Holding her while she cried was only the first step into
the emotional abyss. I have watched television—especially
old movies—enough to know that parents hold children,
and then ultimately children hold parents, while they cry. I
might even have envied the experience. I wasn't sure about
that.

In any case, I couldn't remember sharing it. I occasionally cried, everybody does, but I hadn't been much of a cryer as a child, and Ramona hadn't been much of a comforter as a mother. I admit to having shown up on her doorstep in need of help. But I wasn't crying. And I didn't need to be held. I was sturdy, damn it.

The truly terrible part was that I knew she was, too.

If she had crumbled, and she had, this was without question the worst experience she had ever been through.

Ramona loved Al. No matter how I felt about him. And she couldn't cope with the possibility of losing him.

What had become clear to me in the past four hours was that I couldn't cope with the possibility of her losing him, either.

Ramona had never lived alone, not ever, in her fifty-plus years. If Al didn't pull through, she was planning to sleep on my living room couch for the rest of her life.

Moving her from the porch to the sofa and fixing her tea had taken an hour. First, I had to listen to the story, how Al had thought he had a bad case of indigestion after dinner, but when the pains started radiating to his left arm, she insisted that he go to the hospital. He wouldn't hear of calling an ambulance, and she didn't want to trust the small hospital at the lake with anything more serious than a sprained ankle anyway. So she had driven him from Lake Tahoe to Reno, at night, over the twisting, two-lane Mount Rose highway, as his pains got worse.

When they got to St. Mary's, the emergency room doctor gave her hell. Al could have died in the car.

Ramona had stayed with him in the emergency room

and waited outside the intensive care unit until the nurses began looking sideways at her. When she was reasonably certain he was going to live, she had driven over to find me. She didn't know how long she had been sitting on the porch.

After the tea and the story, she fell asleep. I wanted her to take the bed, but she closed her eyes and stayed put on the couch. I pulled the extra blanket out of the closet and wrapped her in it.

Then I went back out to my office to make phone calls.

The still-blinking light on the answering machine hit me with another bucketful of cold guilt. All three messages were from Ramona. She had called once from Lake Tahoe, when she was still calm. She had tried again from the emergency room, after her voice had begun to quiver. The third time she called she had cracked.

And I had been with Curtis, oblivious. Which wasn't anybody's fault, damn it. The guilt wavered on the edge of anger but didn't quite make it across.

I left a message on Deke's machine, telling him that I had taken the job with Aaron Hiller and Roger Wade, that I had planned to catch up with him at dinner, that Ramona was with me. More when I could.

I found Curtis in his office at the university. I had only planned to try his apartment. And I don't think I would have had him paged at the television station.

But I wanted to let him know what happened and hear his reaction at the same time. And I didn't want to sit by the phone waiting for him to return the call.

"My mother's here," I said. My voice was detached, as

if it were coming from someone sitting next to me. "Al—her husband—had a heart attack."

"I'm sorry. Is he going to make it?"

"She thinks so."

"How are you?"

Hearing his concern helped. I shut my eyes and held the phone hard against my ear.

"Feeling guilty as hell for not being available when she called from the emergency room. Other than that, I'm not sure yet."

"I can be there in half an hour."

"You don't have to do that." The detachment had faltered a little, but the voice still wasn't quite mine.

"Would you rather be alone with your mother? I'll understand if you don't want me to come."

"No, God no, I don't want to be alone with her. I don't know how I'm going to survive being alone with her if she stays for very long. I'll see you in half an hour. And thanks."

I hung up the phone expecting to feel guiltier. For some reason, I felt relieved of a burden instead.

Ramona was still asleep, and I was still huddled at my desk, when Curtis arrived. Butch had calmed down enough to wait with me, but he bolted from my lap at the sound of Curtis's step on the porch. I used to be glad he was such a skilled early warning system. Now I was going to have to try to alter his behavior. Not now. Later. Sometime.

I was stiff as Curtis tried to hug me. Nothing would bend.

"You don't have to let her stay, you know that," he said.

"You're wrong. You're not wrong often, but this time you are. I have to let her stay."

"Okay."

He released me, and I stepped back, not certain what came next. His face was pale with worry, and I suspected I looked like hell.

"Do you want tea or anything?" I asked.

We were still standing by the door. I tried to think of where we could sit. With Ramona in the living room, it would have to be here in the office.

"No. Not unless you're making it for yourself."

I shook my head. "I took the job with Aaron Hiller."

His forehead wrinkled, as if the leap puzzled him. It made sense to me. I didn't want to talk about Ramona.

"And?"

"He says he didn't do it. I don't like him much, and his attorney is an asshole, but I took the job."

"And you think your mother might get in the way?"

"Hell." I rested my forehead against his shoulder.

"Even if she's staying here, you don't have to baby-sit. Give her a key, let her go back and forth to the hospital alone." He put an arm around me and steered me toward one of the two folding chairs in front of the desk.

"What if he dies?"

I plopped down heavily. Curtis took the other chair. He leaned over and picked up my hand. The chairs were too low, and there wasn't really enough room for our legs.

"If you're worried about your mother, you can help her

deal with it if it happens. If you're concerned about Al, you might want to go see him."

"I don't even like him. But I don't want him to die."

"Well, I should hope not!" Ramona was standing in the doorway. Her face was still puffy, even down to her professionally sculpted chin, and her hair was disheveled, but her shoulders were square again.

"I'm sorry. I didn't know you were awake."

"I was never really asleep. I heard voices, and I wanted to see who was here."

I introduced her to Curtis. As he walked over to shake her hand and offer her his chair, she underwent the kind of transformation that I thought only happened in the movies, and then only to Vivien Leigh or Bette Davis. Her eyes widened, her lips trembled, and she forced a tragic smile.

Ramona became the fragile, helpless belle in need of the kindness of strangers.

Curtis almost bowed as he smiled back. For a second, I thought he was going to kiss her fingertips.

Mutual adoration at first sight.

Curtis convinced her that he should take us all out for something that was either a late lunch or an early dinner, since neither Ramona nor I had eaten.

And the truth is, I was grateful for his presence, even grateful for the fuss they were making over each other. If he hadn't been there, she wouldn't have made an effort to recover, and I would in all likelihood have ended up angry and shouting at her, once I had exhausted my ability to deal with her pain.

After a quick meal at a motel coffee shop on Virginia,

we dropped off Ramona at St. Mary's. I told her I'd pick her up at the end of visiting hours.

"She's an amazing woman," Curtis volunteered as he drove me home.

"I'm glad you think so," I said.

"I can see why you clash with her. You're both stubborn and strong-willed."

"Oh, God, Curtis. This is not the moment to tell me I'm like my mother."

He glanced over to determine that I was only annoyed, not angry.

"Okay. But if you really intend to let her stay with you while Al is in the hospital, you might want to make some kind of plan for dealing with her."

"You're suggesting that making it up as I go along won't work?"

"It might. It might also precipitate a crisis that you don't want and don't need to have."

"I'll think about it."

When he pulled up behind Ramona's Oldsmobile, still parked in front of the house, I thanked him for coming and kissed him good-bye.

He was right. I needed a plan. I needed to figure out how I was going to do the job for Aaron Hiller, spend some time in what I hoped was a growing relationship with Curtis, and live with my mother, all at once.

I couldn't plan in the house, and a walk in Wingfield Park wasn't going to do it. I wanted real perspective.

So I drove to the airport and told Jerry McIntire, my buddy at the charter service, that I was taking the

Cherokee 180 for a short flight, just up and back. He signed me out without asking questions.

Even the ritual of the walkaround—draining fuel sumps, checking tires, propeller, oil level, fuel tanks, and control surfaces, then disconnecting the tie-downs—helped dissipate the muddle in my brain.

By the time I was cleared for take-off, taxiing south-east along the runway, feeling the surge of power in my hands, the rush to my heart as the plane lifted, I was almost cheerful again.

Watching the sunset from the level of the mountain tops completed the process. The sky went from bright orange in the clefts between the indigo peaks to pink to pale blue at midheaven. The wings of the Cherokee had a reflected pink glow that made me feel camouflaged in space.

By the time I had circled from the edge of the desert around the city to the foothills, I had an idea that I hoped would save me from disaster. A plan.

I called clearance control to let them know I was ready to land.

I stayed calm as the landing gear thunked gently onto the concrete, and I taxied slowly back to the corner where the Cherokee belonged. I began to get excited when I tied the plane down.

Jerry McIntire waved me on from his spot behind the counter, when he saw that I was in a hurry. I drove the Jeep out of the small parking lot, maneuvered through the airport traffic, and ended up on Plumb Lane. Instead of heading toward home, though, I drove to Virginia and turned north to Court. I stopped in front of Helen Stern's home.

The familiar note was tacked to the door. I waited in the small library for what felt like an hour before I heard her say goodnight to her client.

She sighed heavily when she saw me.

"This is the last time. No more showing up unannounced. After this, you call before coming over and we meet at my convenience. Do you understand?"

"I understand. But I thought you'd want to know that I've been hired by Aaron Hiller's attorney to help with his defense."

Her eyes narrowed until the shadowy circles underneath were all I could see. "You're right. I want to know. Why are you doing it?"

"I could get into a deep philosophical discussion about that. The simplest answer is that I want to stay involved, and he's paying me."

"If he's paying you, what do you want from me?"

"You'll be subpoenaed, by one side or the other, you know that. Sooner or later, you'll have to either talk about Darla Hayden or face down a grand jury over a constitutional issue of whether professional confidence extends to the grave, which will consume time, energy, and money." I wasn't sure that was true, but it sounded good. Helen Stern looked doubtful, so I continued before she could interrupt. "I'd like to know now if there's anything you haven't told me, anything that would prove Aaron's innocence. Or his guilt, for that matter. I'd also like to know if you have information that might implicate anyone else."

"You'll be taking Aaron Hiller's money. How do I know I can trust you?"

"I'm willing to offer a hostage." I was standing, having gotten out of the mustard armchair when she walked in. I sat back down, not wanting to loom over her. "My mother's husband had a heart attack. She needs somebody to talk to, and I'm not a good choice, for a lot of reasons. I think you might be. And it won't be barter— she can afford to pay you."

"Oh, my." Helen Stern laughed softly, clasping her hands beneath her chin. "You'll trust me with your mother, in exchange for Darla Hayden. Is your profession always more important than your primary relationships?"

I ignored that. "I'm not asking for any kind of guarantee. And I haven't mentioned it to her."

"Well, that's the next step, isn't it?" Her hands moved to her cheeks, as if she were holding down a smile. "Ask your mother what she wants to do. And then call me."

She sounded so sensible that I couldn't argue with her.

I was feeling a little deflated as I drove Arlington to Sixth, then pulled into St. Mary's parking lot. I had loved the idea, and I had hoped for a better response from Helen Stern. Even though she was right. I probably should have checked with Ramona first.

But talking to Helen Stern was easier than talking to Ramona. And the next thing I had to do was brave the hospital, which I didn't want to do, and find something nice to say to Al.

Shit.

I cowered as I walked through the glass doors into the white-on-white reception area. There's a nonhuman aura that permeates hospitals, as if something essential is altered when a person is hooked to a machine. I felt depersonalized simply by being there.

A smiling volunteer with a plain, round face framed by short gray hair—unarguably a human being—told me that Al was out of intensive care and gave me directions to his room. I wondered if she were a nun, from one of the orders that had given up habits.

I rode up in the elevator with my eyes closed, praying this wouldn't last long.

Al was in a semiprivate room, in the bed next to the door. He was a big man, with a rectangular face and a bit of a paunch, but lying there made him look flattened, as if his flesh had partly dissolved into the mattress. His sparse hair and abnormally pale skin blurred with the white sheets into the monochrome. The plastic tube of an IV unit trailed to his left hand. He fluttered the fingers of his right one in silent greeting.

Brief, disjointed bursts of words that passed for television dialogue filtered through the curtain separating him from his roommate.

"How're you doing?" I asked.

"Okay." His voice was so faint that even the muted television overwhelmed it.

"Great. I was glad to hear you were out of intensive care."

He blinked.

"I told Ramona I'd pick her up at the end of visiting hours," I added.

"Bathroom," he whispered.

"Oh."

We looked at each other. We had fought when I lived with them my last year of high school, and we hadn't talked much after I moved out. I tried to come up with something that would fill the empty space.

"I'm not angry anymore" was the best I could do.

"Good. Me neither."

I was still struggling to find more words when Ramona emerged from the bathroom. She had spent some time on her hair and makeup and looked her old self, in control.

"Oh, good," she said. "I was afraid you'd be late."

"Yes, well, I'm not." And I had just said I wasn't angry anymore. I forced myself to remember that.

She held Al's hand for a moment, kissed his cheek, and assured him she'd be back in the morning.

We walked down the hall and rode the elevator to the lobby in silence. Ramona had closed her eyes, her energy fading now that she was no longer keeping up Al's spirits. I was trying to come up with a way to suggest she see a therapist.

"I liked Curtis," she said, once we were in the Jeep and on our way.

"He liked you, too."

"I don't want to get in your way. Would you rather I stayed in a hotel?"

"Not tonight." I couldn't have handled the guilt if I'd dropped her off at a hotel. "We could see how it goes with Al the next couple of days, see how long you'll need to be in Reno."

"Thank you."

She fell silent again. That was a measure of how tired

she was. I couldn't remember the last time I had ridden with Ramona in silence.

Since she wasn't trying to talk to me, I couldn't ask her to talk to Helen Stern instead.

"Are you hungry?" I asked instead. Actually, I was hungry. "If so, we have to stop."

"I don't want to go in anywhere," she answered. "Take-out chicken would be fine."

I left her in the car while I picked up enough at a Pioneer franchise so that we could share with the cats and still have some for lunch the next day if necessary.

Her head was against the window when I returned.

The silence lasted until I had parked the Jeep in the driveway, until we were walking up the steps to the house, until we were inside and I broke it.

"I think you ought to take the bed. Let me sleep on the couch. It's my couch."

"You've had it since your first apartment, and you ought to think about replacing it. It was secondhand then." She paused long enough to soften her tone. "You can't sleep on that couch. Your legs are too long. And you have to be fresh tomorrow, for that case you're working on. The murdered girl at the university."

I didn't argue with her.

We ate a little chicken sitting next to each other on the couch, while the small television set—something else left from my first apartment—buffered the silence. Butch and Sundance thought it was a holiday, each having a person solely devoted to slipping him cat-size bites under the coffee table.

While I stowed the leftovers in the refrigerator, she put

together a sleeping space of blankets and pillows. I brought her a T-shirt to sleep in. She hadn't even packed an overnight bag before driving Al to the hospital.

"Are you sure you're okay here?" I asked.

Ramona waved me away. "Get some rest."

I could still hear the electronic murmur of the television when I was ready for bed. Butch was dancing on the blanket, delighted that I was settling in and that Sundance had chosen to stay with Ramona. I flicked on the larger, newer television at my feet to watch the Channel 12 news.

Brianne McKinley was back at her desk. No extended vacation. I suspected the ratings would soar. In a gesture toward propriety, she neither read nor commented on Darla Hayden's murder. Lane Josten informed viewers that Aaron Hiller had an attorney—accompanied by a shot of Hiller and Wade leaving the police station—but that no arrest had been made, and the police had nothing to say. There was a shot of Matthews saying, "No comment." Cut to a shot of David Guerin, the district attorney, saying, "We'll bring charges when we're ready. We're putting the case together now." Mark Martin had a live report from the university, which was as dark and quiet as one would expect it to be at night. This was deceptive, he told us, since another student demonstration was planned for the next day.

The two televisions were in sync past the news, through Jay Leno's opening monologue.

But even when I turned the set off and the house was quiet, I knew she was there.

# Chapter 10

I WOKE THE next morning to the sounds of Ramona in the bathroom, brushing her teeth with the toothbrush she had picked up from the hospital pharmacy, then taking a shower. I finally got up when she moved to the kitchen.

I stopped to take my own turn in the bathroom, and by the time I reached the kitchen, Butch and Sundance had beaten me to it. Ramona had neatly arranged paper towels under their newly filled dishes.

"I'm just fixing a quick cup of coffee," she said. "Then I'll be out of your way."

She had also picked up makeup in the hospital pharmacy. The blush was a little too red, the mascara a little too black for the pallor of her skin. I wondered if she would have looked better without it, just letting the few fine lines the plastic surgeon hadn't erased show how tired she was. I also knew that whatever I thought about the virtues of plainness, she would disagree.

"No problem," I told her. "There's bread in the freezer if you want toast. And thanks for feeding the cats."

"I'm not hungry yet." She was compulsively wiping

157

the counter with a paper towel. She kept it in her hand when the microwave dinged. "I'll pick up something in the hospital cafeteria."

"Okay." I moved past her to get another mug from the plastic drainer beside the sink. I hadn't gotten around to putting them away from the last time I had washed dishes. But at least I had washed the dishes. "I'll be in and out today. I'll give you a key so you can come back whenever you want."

"I may go home tonight. I'll let you know. At some point I have to change clothes, and tonight may be a good time to do that." She smiled fleetingly.

"Okay," I said again. "Leave a message on the machine so I won't wait up for you."

She managed a half-laugh. "I promise to drive carefully."

We stayed at that level, polite, if a little distant, until she left for the hospital.

I settled into my office with a second cup of coffee, checked my E-mail, and made a couple of phone calls.

Jeannie Hiller would see me at eleven, Brianne McKinley at two. She wasn't happy about it, but she agreed to fit me in. I just had time to check with Matthews on my way to the Hiller residence.

I drove the short distance to the police station parking lot, since I'd be heading north from there. The Hillers lived in the same quadrant of town that the university was in. Not what I would have expected. Professors who had been in Reno a long time lived there, but newer ones had tended to buy in the southwest section of town, an area that had been reserved for Old Money until growth had made the privacy of the surrounding foothills decidedly more attractive and the brick houses they left behind more affordable.

Verdi would be a boomtown yet.

Matthews was on his way out the door as I started up the stairs. He stopped a step above me so that we were eye to eye.

"Make it quick," he said. "What have you got?"

"Hiller and Wade have hired me for the defense. I don't want to get in your way, and I hope we can cooperate."

"Jesus, O'Neal." He shook his head slowly, heavy jowls following half a beat late. "First I see you wearing makeup and getting along with a guy, now I see you working for a murderer. I would have gone broke betting against both. What's next?"

"I make the Jack of Spades jump out of a deck of cards and spit cider in your ear. Wanna bet on that?"

"Not today." He started to edge past me.

"Why do you think Hiller's guilty?"

"Why did you take the case?"

"Presumption of innocence. Unless you can prove otherwise."

"Bull. You wanted to stay involved, that's all. And I'll bet on that." Matthews hitched his shoulders as if he were getting ready for a standoff. "I gotta go, but I'll tell you this much. The deceased had consensual intercourse with a man shortly before her death. Somebody slapped her around while she was alive, then hit her with a blunt instrument repeatedly, more than enough blows to kill her. Murder weapon wasn't at the scene. A DNA sample can clear your employer. Or not. He doesn't want to give it. Won't even offer a blood type. And we don't have any evidence to put anybody other than Hiller and the victim in the office that night. Thurman's prints were on the door jamb. I guess you and your boyfriend didn't touch anything. Okay?"

"Yeah, sort of. Aaron could have fucked her without killing her, you know that. Even fucked her and slapped her without killing her." I was annoyed that Aaron hadn't been more forthcoming. He hadn't mentioned inter-course.

Matthews grinned, as if he read my mind.

"Right. See you later."

He hurried down the steps, his feet barely keeping up with his beer belly.

I trudged back to the Jeep. Aaron would have to open up if he wanted me to stay. I wanted to know more about what had happened in his office that night. If he had screwed her. If he had slapped her. If he had killed her. No more letting abstract questions about theoretical rights get in the way of simple truths.

And I knew I would have insisted on getting those answers already if I hadn't been distracted by my own life. If I hadn't wanted to hold onto the case. If I hadn't been fascinated by all the hype—even been part of it in a moment of raccoon-eyed madness.

There were too damn many hedges, qualifiers, and conditional statements floating around. And underneath them all, there was a murderer.

If it was Aaron Hiller, I wanted him to fry. It made no difference that I knew him.

At least I didn't want knowing him to make a difference.

Shit.

That's why the law is supposed to be impersonal. Knowing people—even when you don't like them— could affect your judgment.

The rumination took me all the way to Seventh Street, to the curve onto University Terrace, and almost all the way to Peavine. When I was young, I had thought of Peavine as a stark, sandy mountain, sparsely dotted with sagebrush, at the edge of civilization. Now I saw it as nothing more than a barren hill, with houses climbing halfway up.

The address I was looking for turned out to be a dark-frame ranch house on the south side of the peak. Junipers ran from the street up the edge of the driveway and partially obscured the stone veneer that protected the house up to the snow level.

I parked behind a blue Ford Taurus.

Jeannie Hiller met me at the door.

Even though I knew she had once been Aaron's student, her youth hadn't really registered when I saw her at the faculty reception. She was maybe five years older than Darla Hayden, maybe the same age as Brianne McKinley. And as different from each of them—physically, at least—as they were from each other.

Jeannie's dark brown hair hung in a straight bob that didn't quite hit her shoulders. Her skin was clear, with only a touch of mascara showing around wide brown eyes. She was wearing khakis, a T-shirt, and a woolly green cardigan that might have belonged to Aaron.

The real difference, though, was something I'd have to call aura. Where Darla was frantic, and Brianne energetic, as if they had popcorn emanating from their nerve ends, Jeannie was calm. Oddly calm, considering the circumstances.

"Would you mind taking off your boots? They tear up the tatami mats," she said.

I did mind, but I didn't argue. I left them on the porch and followed her into the sunken living room.

The tatami mats covered what felt to my stockinged feet like a hardwood floor. Folded futons and low enamel tables were the only furnishings. The wall space was almost entirely filled with painted screens and hanging silks of tigers, in all their black and orange and white splendor, some snarling and ferocious, some quiet and nurturing with cubs. I was reminded of the Japanese wing of a museum. Aaron Hiller had either spent a lot of time in Japan or a lot of money at import shops.

"Can I offer you anything?" Jeannie Hiller asked.

When I declined, she gracefully lowered herself to one of the futons, legs pulled up neatly. I imitated her as best I could. A black bowl of carefully arranged yellow and white chrysanthemums decorated an otherwise empty table between us.

"I was impressed by your bravery at the faculty reception," she said. "And so was Aaron. I was a little surprised when he told me he had hired a female private investigator, but not after I knew who you were."

"I'm not having an affair with him," I replied.

She laughed, not bothered in the least. "No, of course not. You were with Curtis Breckinridge the other night.

Besides, if Aaron were interested in you, he would have talked you out of calling me. Told you that I couldn't provide an alibi, but I had one of my own. Assured you that I wasn't jealous, but nothing could be gained by confronting me."

"True?"

"Yes, actually. There was an antique show at the convention center. I went with a friend who collects early American dolls. We stayed until it closed at seven, because she was hoping for last-minute bargains, then we had dinner together. I came straight home after that. Aaron was here, but I'm not certain what time that was. I didn't check." She managed to look both sad and sincere, as if she was really sorry she couldn't be of more help.

"What about the jealousy?"

"There's no point." Her face was still open, her words soft. I almost missed the tug at the sweater, pulling it across her body.

"I don't understand."

"If I were jealous, I wouldn't have time or space for anything else. Aaron would have been far happier in a religion that condoned polygamy, a society that approved of harems. Or at least one where men are expected to have concubines. He likes to be surrounded by women. He falls in love with them spontaneously, completely, and often. When he falls out of love, he moves on. But he continues to cherish, in his own self-centered way, every past object of affection." She leaned forward and smiled, elbows on her knees, as if she were talking about a beloved child. "To be jealous, I would have to feel threatened."

"Instead, you do the threatening."

"Oh, dear, no." She shook her head. "If you're thinking of Mary Beth, Aaron's first wife, she was always jealous, always threatened—long before I came along—until finally she left him. If she had waited a little longer, he would have been out of love with me and home again. At least until he targeted someone else. But he *was* in love with me, and I was the one who bandaged the wound to his ego when she moved out, so he married me. And as long as I don't move out, he'll always come home to me. Someone has to be here to take care of him."

"Why couldn't any one of the others do that just as well?"

"In theory, I suppose one could. In practice, he wouldn't want the upheaval of leaving me. And he has enough insight into his own psyche to realize that replacing me with his current infatuation, no matter how attractive she might be, wouldn't necessarily be a long-term improvement." Her smile turned smug.

"Did you know about Darla Hayden?" I considered asking about Brianne, too, but that would have felt mean.

"Not specifically. Not at the time, anyway." She couldn't hold on to the smile. "I knew Aaron had been seeing someone at the university, because he came up with a series of excuses to keep me away from social situations where wives were included, where I would have expected to have been included. She had to be either a colleague or a graduate student."

"You weren't curious?"

"No." Her face was too smooth. "I knew it was over when he started inviting me again. And I knew from his discomfort that whoever-she-was hadn't accepted a clean break. When she circulated the memos to the faculty, he had to tell me before someone else did. That wasn't easy for him."

"He said she was stalking him."

"Well, I wouldn't call it that." She found the indulgent smile again. "Stalking sounds a bit dramatic. She did send him a birthday card. For some reason, it upset him. Otherwise he would have passed it off as meaningless."

"Then you did know about Darla Hayden before she showed up in the faculty center with a toy gun."

Jeannie started tugging at the sweater again.

"I'd seen her. Of course I'd seen her. The department is too small, and Aaron couldn't keep me away from everything. She would stare at me, with those haunted eyes, and I prayed she wasn't staring like that because Aaron—" She shut her own eyes, cutting off a glimpse of whatever ghosts were there. She reopened them and continued firmly. "I knew Darla Hayden was Aaron's student. He always has bright women doctoral students. He likes to help their careers."

I almost interrupted, but I managed to keep my mouth shut.

"And whatever happened, I don't know why she had to send those memos. That was cruel, to go after him like that," she added.

"You don't think Aaron might have been cruel to her?"

Jeannie's jaw dropped. "No. I'm sorry, but I don't. Aaron isn't a cruel man. Thoughtless sometimes, even insensitive, but not cruel. Whatever you've heard is wrong." She paused, as if wondering what I'd heard. Her voice was under control when she spoke again. "I'm sorry for her, too, I really am. But I didn't know her, and I just don't know anything that could help you find her killer."

"Okay. Thanks for your time." More questions right then would have been hostile, if not cruel. And I was still working for her husband.

"You're going?" Her voice was bright with relief.

"Yeah." I stood up. "If you don't know anything, I'd better find someone who does. I charge by the hour."

"Oh. Yes. I'm sure someone else will know something. Randy Thurman was close to the whole messy situation— Aaron told me that after the Friday night episode. And it's been so long since Aaron was involved with her, she might have been seeing someone else. Someone must have a better motive to kill her than Aaron does." She stopped herself and rose from the futon, again graceful and smiling, the calm if casual hostess once more. "As soon as this is resolved, we plan to give a party. You'll have to come again then."

I suspected I would see her before the party, if there ever was one, but I politely said good-bye.

I had to stop on the porch to put my boots back on.

"One more thing," Jeannie added from the doorway. Her face was mottled from a sudden spike in her heartbeat, and she was hugging herself, embracing herself in Aaron's sweater. "I wasn't going to mention this—it's a little embarrassing, really—but I know Aaron didn't see anyone else Sunday evening. We made love that night, and Aaron never makes love with me if he has spent the evening with someone else. Don't tell anyone. Please. I just wanted you to understand why I'm so certain someone else had to have been in his office."

"Thanks for letting me know," I said. I fought the urge to ask if he'd slapped her around as foreplay. "I'll treat it as confidential if at all possible."

"Good." Her face cleared again. She stayed in the doorway until I had backed the Jeep out of the driveway and started down the hill.

I didn't believe her about making love. Maybe they had, maybe they hadn't. But I would have bet the ranch she knew that Aaron had screwed somebody else earlier that evening. And Aaron—or Matthews—had told her somebody screwed Darla Hayden.

The campus would have blocked a beeline from the Hiller residence to the television station even if I hadn't wanted to stop. I could check out the demonstration. I could see if Randy Thurman was around. And I could see if Curtis wanted to have lunch.

I parked in the lot behind the old gym and walked past the library to the business school. When I didn't see a news van, I figured I was early for the demonstration.

First Thurman, then Curtis, then the quad. Except I headed toward the management side, not finance, when I entered the building.

The door to Curtis's office was closed, and nothing happened when I knocked. I didn't realize how much I wanted to see him until the disappointment set in.

I retraced my steps and took the hall to the finance department.

"Professor Thurman left for an early lunch," the long-haired receptionist told me. "But he'll be back in time for the demonstration."

She barely repressed a giggle. It could have come from nerves, but it was a giggle nonetheless.

"What's funny about the demonstration?"

"Nothing." She quickly composed herself. "It's just that Rick has been moaning for over a year about how grad students are treated, and nobody's paid any attention. Now he's on television."

"Who's Rick?"

"Rick Rodriguez." She glanced down as if she might have made a mistake.

"Was he making a speech at the statue on Monday?"

She looked back at me and nodded. "And he's making another one today."

"What can you tell me about him?" I perched on the corner of her desk, settling in for a while.

"He's getting a Ph.D. in English. His dissertation is on nineteenth-century Gothic fiction, focusing on the vampires, especially Polidori and Le Fanu and the other predecessors to Stoker's *Dracula*."

It was my turn to repress a giggle.

"I guess you know him pretty well," I said.

"I do—but his work is fascinating on its own." She leaned forward and looked up at me. "Rick sees the vampire myth as a political metaphor for the giant corporations that live forever by draining the blood of the people who work for them. The way universities drain the blood of graduate students."

I resisted the urge to point out to her that giant

corporations don't live forever and that the politics sounded as nineteenth-century as the fiction.

"Did he ever get together with Darla Hayden?"

She nodded solemnly, appraising me before she answered. "When I gave him copies of the memos she sent to the faculty, he tried to get her to join the movement to unionize the graduate students, but she didn't want to do it. Darla bought into all that free market, meritocratic crap, you know. She just didn't understand that most of us can't negotiate our own contracts—most of us need group support." The phone rang, and she took a break to answer it. As soon as she got rid of the caller, she was back. "Have you seen her memos?"

"A couple of them. And you're right, she wanted to negotiate her own contract." I was dealing with a left-wing Jeannie Hiller, her life caught up in someone else's work. "I'm sorry, but we haven't been introduced. I'm Freddie O'Neal, and I'm a private investigator."

I thought about extending my hand, but I didn't.

"I know who you are. You were here to see Professor Thurman last week. You were with Professor Breckinridge when Darla's body was discovered. And the rumor is that Professor Hiller hired you to help with his defense." She smiled like a first-time poker player who was just dealt a straight flush in five-card stud.

"Hey, that's good. And you are . . .?"

"Gabriela Rodriguez. Pleased to meet you."

Gabriela extended her hand, and I shook it.

"Pleased to meet you, too. Related to Rick?"

"He's my brother."

"Great. What else do you know?"

She blinked. Maybe I should have been more subtle. "You mean about Rick?"

"Or about Darla."

"About Darla," she repeated, appraising me again. "When she was a student, she never had time to talk to secretaries. She didn't talk much to Rick or the other grad students, either. We can only guess that she talked to Professor Hiller." She hesitated to make sure I was going to smile at her little joke. "Maybe I can find a memo or something you don't have. If I do, I'll copy it for you."

"One I don't have?"

"Yeah—you probably have the public ones, but if one went just to Professor Thurman, you might not have it. I'll see."

Before I could thank her, Thurman was in the doorway. Everything about him seemed slightly askew, including his tie and his glasses. One long-fingered hand tried to smooth the sparse hair along his broad, ashen forehead.

"I can't talk to you now," he said, skipping right past a greeting. "The news vans have arrived. I have to meet with the president, the public information director, and the university's attorney. We're trying to come up with a way that we can ban camera coverage of student activities."

"I don't think you can repeal the First Amendment in the next ten minutes," I told him.

"No. But there has to be some way to keep that raving maniac of a graduate student from exploiting this tragedy for his own ends. I'm not putting you off—Aaron told me he had hired you, and I'll do whatever I can to help.

Tomorrow would be better. I can talk with you tomorrow." Thurman turned to Gabriela. "I'll be going straight to the quad from the president's office, and I don't know what time I'll be back. Do the best you can to keep the office functioning."

He disappeared into the hall.

"Raving maniac," Gabriela mocked. "Rick is just exploiting his exploiters. I wish I could go hear him."

If Thurman knew Rick was her brother, she had a right to be angry.

"Tell you what. I'll report back afterward."

"Hey, thanks, I'll look for the memo."

The phone rang again. I left as Gabriela answered it.

By the time I reached the door to the building, three news vans were lined up in front, cables snaking toward the quad. Curtis was standing next to Mark Martin near the one labeled Channel 12 News.

His face changed as he saw me walking over. I got self-conscious and stopped about two feet farther away from him than I'd intended.

"I guess you've already had lunch," I said to Curtis. I nodded hello to Mark, who nodded back.

"Yes." Curtis's brow furrowed, as if I might not forgive him. "I'd go with you anyway, but I really want to see what's happening here."

"Okay. I'll pick up a sandwich from the cafeteria and bring it back."

I slipped between the vans and crossed over to the student union. Not to be confused with unionizing students. Rick Rodriguez had taken on a fool's task. Trying to organize a union in Nevada, one of the staunch right-to-work states, would have been hard enough if he'd been talking to prison guards. No way would he get anywhere with students. Too many of them came from the cow counties, where the Old West and the spirit of self-determination were alive and kicking and a lot more powerful than vampires.

The basement cafeteria was crowded with students who either didn't know about the demonstration or didn't care. I grabbed a wrapped sandwich, tuna on white, picked up a bag of potato chips, and cut to the head of the line. A football player glared, but I glared back and he let me go.

I ate the sandwich as I walked back up the stairs and tossed the plastic wrapper into a litter bin at the curb. I was halfway through the potato chips by the time I found Curtis. He was standing under a tree near the business school, right about where we had been on Monday. I held out the bag, but he shook his head.

Mark and his two competitors, complete with crews sprouting equipment at odd angles, were closer to Rick Rodriguez and the Mackay statue than the score or so of students, most of whom seemed more interested in the cameras than in Rick. He and the three students behind him, dressed in uniforms of jeans and blue work shirts, conferred for a minute. Then Rick stepped in front of the statue, held a bullhorn to his mouth, and called, "Could I have your attention? Could I have your attention?"

A young woman in the same jeans and work shirt rushed up with some signs. Two said "Arrest Aaron Hiller!" and a third "Avenge Darla Hayden!" She passed them to the other members of the chorus and started waving "Solidarity Now!"

When he was certain the cameras were rolling, Rick Rodriguez started his speech. The prologue sounded like a repeat of what we had heard on Monday. But he took off in a new direction—and began to get the attention he had asked for—when he began to describe Darla Hayden's bruised and battered body.

"She was found dead—murdered—not ten yards from where I stand," he shouted. "The woman, the colleague, the fellow student who suffered what we have suffered— and more—bled to death in the office of the man who had exploited her in life. But has he been arrested? Has he been charged? No! And why not? Why is Aaron Hiller still free? Because Aaron Hiller is powerful, and Darla Hayden was not."

"Murder weapon," one of the watching students called out.

"Murder weapon?" Rick Rodriguez's voice was distorted by the poor amplification. The sound men must have been going nuts. "The real murder weapon was power—power was the blunt instrument that killed Darla Hayden and keeps her murderer free. But if the police want proof, let them ask the right question, and let them demand an answer: What is missing from Aaron Hiller's office?"

Whatever Rick Rodriguez had planned to say next was lost in an ear-splitting electronic wail emanating from Morrill Hall. The administration had just repealed the First Amendment.

# Chapter 11

THE CURE HAD to have been worse than the disease. The alarm had stopped both Rick Rodriguez and the news crews, at least temporarily. But as it continued to pulse emergency shrieks across the campus, students started streaming out of buildings to see what was going on.

"Is that an old air raid siren?" Curtis leaned over and spoke directly into my ear so that he didn't have to shout.

"Maybe, but I'd bet it's from the fifties. An early cold war A-bomb alert, so students could crouch under their desks in case of Communist attack." Mouth to ear was the only way to be understood. "Rick and the sign wavers are probably as close to Commies as the current boys at the top have seen. I'm surprised Thurman went along, though."

Curtis didn't answer. He tugged at my arm and pointed to the end of the quad, where Randy Thurman was apparently shouting in vain at a man in a navy-blue suit, who had to be the president of the university. I hadn't met him, but I had seen him on television, offering a "No comment" to the camera. I was sorry he hadn't listened to Thurman's counsel.

When I turned back to the statue, Mark Martin, the two other field reporters, and the three sound engineers were retreating to their vans. The three camera operators were still shooting the crowd. Rick Rodriguez and his small army had disappeared from the battlefield.

The siren stopped as abruptly as it had begun.

My ears rang with silence.

I grabbed Curtis's hand and started back toward the business school. By the time we were through the doors and into the hall, I could speak in a normal tone.

"I have to check with the finance secretary, and then leave to meet Brianne at the television station," I said.

"And your mother is staying with you," he added.

"Well, yeah, but that wasn't what I was going to say." I wasn't making an excuse to run off, and I didn't have to defend myself. "Listen, I haven't had a chance to talk with Sandra, to see if she still plans on dinner tomorrow night. But one way or another, I'll see you then."

"I may see you at Channel 12 first."

We parted awkwardly. At least we were both smiling.

The finance office was locked. Gabriela Rodriguez had either taken the emergency alarm seriously or seen it as an excuse to find out for herself what was going on. I would have to wait for the memo. And wait to find out what was missing from Aaron Hiller's office. Someone had to have passed that information to Rick Rodriguez—if something was in fact missing. One more question Aaron Hiller would have to answer when I saw him again.

I threaded my way through the molecular clumps of

THE LUCK OF THE DRAW        177

students, back toward the parking lot. I had to get in line to pull out. The siren had evidently been the signal for all unpoliticized students—which was most of them—to leave campus. I hadn't planned on dropping down to the freeway for the few miles to Wells Avenue, but I was on the verge of being late.

Wells took me to Oddie Boulevard, and I was parking the Jeep in front of the squat gray building with the fat round antenna on top at five to two. I had decided against the lot because a red Corvette was blocking the entrance while the driver talked to someone.

The conferees were Lane Josten and Steve Burns. They were saying good-bye as I walked up. Burns waved and drove off. Josten waited, flashing a toothpaste commercial smile that sparkled against his ski-slope tan. And wearing a clean, soft-blue shirt, just the color of his eyes.

"Sandra told me you're a friend," he said.

"Did you think I was an enemy?"

The smile was infectious. I had to return it.

"I didn't know what you were, except that you had to be interesting. I saw the videotape where you sucker-punched Brianne. And I heard you were involved with Curtis."

"You're way ahead of me. All I know is that Sandra likes you—I hope the sucker punch wasn't betraying a confidence. And Curtis thinks you're easygoing." That sounded better than lacking ambition.

Lane laughed as if he had picked up on the euphemism. "Brianne's affair with Aaron Hiller is gossip, not confidence. And Curtis doesn't understand why I find her amusing. He's all prepared to deal with competitive people, which is why he does so well with Steve and Brianne. I'll bet he plays tennis to win."

Lane Josten was both smarter than I had thought and more engaging than I had expected.

"I don't know. I don't play. But I wouldn't take the bet. And just so I can tell him—why *do* you find Brianne amusing?" My cheeks were beginning to ache from smiling.

"Well, just what is she fighting for? She's the top anchor in Reno. She could kick back and enjoy, but she doesn't."

"And you do."

"Yeah." He clapped a hand on my shoulder. "But I get the job done, too, and right now I gotta go do it."

"Fine. Right now I gotta talk to Brianne. And by the way, thanks for lending me the shirt."

"Anytime. It looked better on you anyway."

It didn't, but I let it go.

Lane escorted me across the parking lot, through the doors, past the receptionist, and down the hall to the newsroom. I had expected something clean and high-tech. What I saw was a clutter of desks, computer terminals, clattering teleprinters, and rolling reams of paper overflowing everywhere.

Brianne glanced away from her screen long enough to register my arrival and then ignored me for the next ten minutes. I was reading an Associated Press story coming off the wire, about jury selection in the Washington, D.C. trial of a man who took a shot at the president, when she tapped me on the shoulder.

"We can't talk in here," she said.

I followed her down the hall, wondering about the point of a trial when three concerned citizens caught the would-be assassin in the act. I was certain Curtis would have an opinion.

Brianne hustled me into the empty makeup room and perched on one of the chairs. I was intimidated before I even opened my mouth. There was no way I could escape our images, reflected in the wall-length mirror above the jumble of round, squat jars and round, long brushes.

Coiffed dark hair, with frankly artificial blond streaks, covered her forehead with a heavy fringe and tapered gracefully below her pointed chin. Her prominent eyes were deep blue, with lashes that seemed to have been waiting for mascara to show off their length. Her bright red mouth had a self-confident smile. A navy-blue silk scarf with red and white stripes that would have looked like a flag on someone else looked commanding on her.

My hazel eyes faded out against pale, freckled skin covering features dominated by a square jaw. The white shirt I was wearing didn't help out with color. I resisted an impulse to pull my denim jacket closed.

But hell, I had her on the hair. Whatever else was going on, that autumn-leaf mane falling over my shoulders looked pretty good. I decided to stand.

"All right," Brianne said, tilting her head up. "I want you to know that Aaron hired you at my suggestion. I thought it would look better if he had a woman on his team, you mentioned in the interview that you did legal work, and you were clearly capable of going for the jugular. Besides, Curtis Breckinridge is a good judge of people. So you must be bright and analytical. He certainly didn't fall in love with your body."

What I thought was, fuck you, even as my head registered that she thought Curtis was in love with me, and my heart registered an extra beat. What I said was, "Why did you fall in love with Aaron Hiller? He seems to go for the powerless types, like his students."

"During the early years of his career, he became involved with students because they were there—and available. Now, they go for him, and he finds the little darlings hard to resist. But Aaron went for me. And I'm not in love with him." Brianne checked her reflection in the mirror. She must have decided that it was flawless, because she clasped her hands on her knees and waited.

"Okay. So why are you sleeping with him?"

"Aaron Hiller is a nationally known expert on the Japanese financial system. Ted Koppel has interviewed him six times on *Nightline*." She paused to let me draw my own conclusion.

"He's your ticket to the network," I said.

"Brava. Or at least to a network-owned station."

"Does he know you're using him?"

I was hoping to get a rise out of her, but the question didn't crack her cool.

"It's not that crass. Aaron and I enjoy each other's company. He expects woman to want something from him—usually it's fidelity or commitment. He's actually relieved that all I want is a few phone calls and a couple of introductions."

"But they won't do you any good if he's in jail for murder."

"No. Which is the only reason I'm talking with you."

I sat down in the chair next to her and swiveled it around so that my back was to the mirror. Enough was enough.

"What do you know?" I asked.

"Aaron came over to see me Sunday night. He told me that Darla Hayden had been in his office." Brianne leaned against the makeup table, after carefully checking to see that the spot her elbow hit was clean. Her voice was as low as a co-conspirator's. "I said he shouldn't have agreed to meet her. He knew that, but he hoped talking to her would help. He was even willing to help her get into another doctoral program if she wanted to leave Reno."

"He's a great guy. Did Darla agree to go?"

"She seemed to believe that there was some sort of principle involved in her fight with the department. She wanted to see it through."

"And?"

"That's all." Brianne shrugged. "Aaron left her there and drove to my place."

"Did he leave her in his office?" I didn't really think Aaron was dumb enough to give two different stories, but I asked anyway.

"No. They said good-bye in front of the building. The killer must have taken her back in. Someone has to have a master key."

"Ah. Of course. Probably several people. I don't suppose Aaron said anything about whether he touched her."

She looked at me as if I had a missing gene. "Aaron

didn't touch her. He didn't beat her, he didn't screw her. I know there's a rumor that he can get a little rough, but it isn't true."

"You're sure he didn't touch her?" If Aaron got a little rough, I could imagine Brianne getting rough right back. They could gut-shoot each other in the name of love, or whatever they wanted to call it.

She squeezed the condescension into a smile. "We didn't spend the whole evening talking. And I can assure you, he didn't do anything with anyone else before or after."

"Funny. That's what his wife said."

I slipped that one in under her guard, and she took a moment before answering.

"Jeannie's lying. She thinks Aaron needs an alibi, and she wants to provide it."

"And you're telling the truth?"

"I'm telling the truth."

"Okay. What else do you know?"

Brianne stood, smoothing her navy-blue skirt. Somewhere a navy-blue jacket was hanging, waiting to be called to duty.

"Nothing that has to do with Darla Hayden, I'm afraid. I hope you can find the killer without a sworn statement from me. If you can't, let me know. In the meantime, I have to get back to work."

She walked out and left me sitting. I guess she figured I knew where the front door was.

There didn't seem to be any point in wandering around the station. I asked the receptionist if Curtis had come in. She said they were expecting him later.

I walked slowly to the Jeep, in case he showed up. And I watched for the Volvo as I retraced Oddie to Wells. When I passed the turn that would have taken me back toward the campus, I shifted mental gears to what I had to do next.

Since Thurman said he'd be available the next day, I could check with Gabriela Rodriguez then, too. What I really needed to do before going any further was to nose around wherever Darla Hayden had moved to. Unless Matthews wanted to give me the address—and he probably didn't—my best bet to get it was Helen Stern.

She had told me not to stop by without calling. I decided I might as well call from home, so I could wait in relative comfort if I reached her machine and needed a return call.

Relative comfort turned out to be a bad pun. Ramona's Oldsmobile was parked in front of my house.

Butch was sitting on the porch step, glaring. He slipped off and hid behind the small lilac bush before I could grab him.

I had planted the lilac in June. I liked lilacs, and the man at the nursery had assured me that they don't need much attention. This one was doing all right. So far.

When I entered my office, my nose was assaulted by a combination of Pledge and Lysol. My eyes were assaulted by straightened books and papers and a vacuumed carpet.

My mother had cleaned my house.

My mother was still cleaning my house, in fact. I found her in the kitchen, wiping the inside of the refrigerator. Beer, butter, cheese, mayonnaise, and mustard sat on the glistening tile counter. I couldn't remember if there had been any other foodstuffs on ice. It didn't matter. They were gone now.

"How long has it been since you defrosted?" she asked.

"I don't know."

"If you just got a frost-free model, you wouldn't have to worry about it."

"Ramona, stop this!"

"What?" She pulled her head out of the refrigerator. Her face looked remarkably fresh, with a little added color from the exertion. But her eyes weren't quite focused. And the black silk blouse that she had been wearing for the last twenty-four hours was starting to go limp.

"You don't have to clean my house. You can be a guest. It's okay."

She took the old towel she had been using over to the sink and held it under the faucet, then wrung it out, before she answered.

"I could tell you were making an effort. I thought maybe it was because of Curtis. And I thought if I got it all clean, it would be easier for you to keep it that way." She turned back toward me, pleading. "You don't have to do everything at once, you know. Just clean it up when you see it, do it when it bothers you."

I couldn't shout at her, couldn't tell her that whatever it had looked like to her, it was mine, and I could live with it.

"I'm doing my best. Thank you for noticing. And thank you for wanting to help. How's Al?"

"A little better. He had a bout of arrhythmia this morning that made everyone nervous. And they have him on some kind of medication that makes him drowsy."

"Sounds like he'll be in for a while."

"Yes." She turned back to the sink.

I walked over and put my arm across her shoulders.

"You can stay as long as you want. I'd just like it if you warn me before you do anything drastic like redecorating."

"I was thinking about replacing the blinds in your bedroom." Her head dropped, copper curls falling forward. "And you really need chairs in your office. For clients."

This was the moment, now or never.

"I know you're stressed, and you want to keep busy, and you still think of me as your kid. And I don't want to fight with you over territory. So would you be willing to talk about it with someone?"

She looked up at me, eyes blank, and I had to continue.

"Ramona, I'm not good at this. I'm not good at meeting other people's emotional needs. I thought it might help if you talked to somebody else. A therapist. She's a really bright woman, and I think you might like her."

"I am not ill," she snapped, eyes focused again. "You're right. I am stressed. I am doing my best to handle it, and I don't need to talk to anyone about it. As far as your house is concerned, I was only trying to help. I'm sorry. I won't do it again."

"Okay." I removed my arm and stepped back. "I'm sorry, too. I guess we were both only trying to help."

She started replacing things in the refrigerator.

"I can finish in a minute. And Al's expecting me to come back before dinner. I told him I'd eat with him tonight. After that, I'm going home."

"I want you to come back tomorrow. Please say you'll come back tomorrow." For a second, I felt like a kid, still needing her approval.

"I don't know." She straightened up and sighed, holding on to the refrigerator door. "If I'm going to have to stay in Reno for any length of time, I'll be more comfortable in a hotel. And you'll be more comfortable, too."

I tried to come up with an answer to that, but I couldn't.

"Well—let me know what you want to do." I retreated to the doorway. "I need to make a couple of phone calls."

She nodded, her back toward me.

When I got to my office, I just sat in my chair, needing to assess the damage and reclaim the space.

Sundance appeared from nowhere and hopped onto my lap. He butted his forehead against my chest and purred. Ramona was in the kitchen, Butch was outside, and all was well with his world. I scratched his ears, and he flopped onto his side, still purring.

I know that some people pay to have other people come in and clean their houses. I never have. I'd rather live with my own disorder than pay someone else to clean it up. The idea is as embarrassing as paying someone to give me a bath would be. I've lived alone too long to be comfortable with that sort of intimacy. It was hard enough for me to accept the kind that comes with love.

And maybe that was the problem. Ramona and I had never been very good at expressing love for each other. Too much had gone wrong—probably starting with Danny, the father whose soul I fervently hope rests in an Irish heaven with free-flowing Bushmills. If it were somebody else's life, somebody else's mother, I would argue that a wound so old would have to be healed. Which just shows how little I know.

Ramona really hadn't done much beyond dusting, vacuuming, and putting a basket under the plant on my desk. She must have picked up the basket at the hospital gift shop, along with her other sundry purchases. I had overreacted with her, one more time.

I looked up Helen Stern's number and picked up the phone. I left a message on her machine. Then I tried Sandra's office and had to leave a message there, too.

I knew Helen Stern had told me not to show up again without warning. But I couldn't sit and wait. I gave Sundance one last pat and dislodged him from my lap, despite his protests.

Ramona was in the living room, putting on her quilted purple jacket. She had folded the blanket and fluffed the pillows on the sofa.

"It was really nice of you to straighten up," I said. "I appreciate your effort."

"Oh, don't." She picked up her patchwork leather bag with the sequined rose. "We've lived such separate lives. I had hoped we could reconnect, but I guess this just isn't the time. The problems between us started with Danny, I know. I thought you'd forgiven me, but I guess I was wrong about that, too. You were just old enough when he left to hold onto the hurt forever."

That stung especially hard because I had been thinking the same thing.

"I'm almost okay about it," I said.

The line struck her as funny. When she laughed—a high, little-girl laugh—I had to laugh, too.

We managed to hug each other before going in separate directions.

I drove to Helen Stern's office thinking about how different life is from television. If Ramona and I were living in a sitcom, my realization that Danny was an alcoholic bum who wouldn't have made either of us happy would have magically fixed everything. And I had really wanted that to happen.

But Ramona and I had fought too often over the years. She had thoughtlessly slashed my self-confidence too many times, and while some of the pain had disappeared, the memories hadn't. I could understand and forgive her—and she could understand and forgive me for fighting back—but we still had a certain wariness with one another that neither of us quite knew how to get over.

I parked the Jeep and walked to the heavy Victorian door thinking that maybe Helen Stern was right about therapy. I couldn't talk to her while I was investigating the case, but maybe when it was over, she could help me work things out with Ramona.

There was no note on the door, but it gave when I lifted and dropped the brass knocker.

"Hello," I called.

When I didn't get an answer, I pushed the door open. She might have simply forgotten to post the note.

The door to the library was open. So was the door to her office.

"Hello," I called again.

She was seated at her desk, leaning at an awkward angle to her left.

"Dr. Stern?"

She didn't answer. And she didn't move as I entered the room.

As I started toward her, I noticed that one of the desk drawers was open. And then I saw the dark red stain splattered low on the wall.

I froze to see what else was going on. The office door swung toward me, almost imperceptibly.

I grabbed the knob and dived back across the threshold, pulling the door with me.

A bullet slammed into the wood.

I dived again, out the front door this time, again pulling it shut behind me. I rolled off the porch onto the lawn and crawled toward one of the massive elms.

The sun was low in the sky, and a light autumn breeze rustled the faded leaves above me. I shivered in the cold, waiting for the next shot.

# Chapter 12

I WAITED UNTIL the sun began to slip behind the mountains. No bullets thudded over my head into the solid trunk.

I didn't even hear a hand rattle the door.

When the silence lasted, and I was too cold to wait any longer, I got up, walked to the attorney's office on the ground floor of the restored Victorian across the street, and asked the secretary to call the police. Helen Stern had had an accident.

I went back outside to wait in my Jeep and watch the front of the house. I held onto the steering wheel to keep my hands steady.

No way was I going toward a closed door with an armed murderer on the other side. If I'd been carrying, I might have slipped around to the back. But both the big Beretta and the miniature All-American that I sometimes carried in my boot were sitting in my bedroom dresser drawer.

I hoped Ramona hadn't found them.

The black-and-white arrived in about five minutes. I

explained to Michelle Urrutia and her partner what had happened.

"Shit, O'Neal, we need backup," she said, reaching for the car radio.

"You know he's gone by now," I answered.

"He? You saw somebody?"

"No. Sorry. An automatic, sexist response."

"You're probably right. On all counts. I'm still calling for help."

"Make it quick," her partner said, drawing his gun. "I'm heading around to the back."

"Hold onto your balls, Knox," Michelle said. "Your bulletproof vest isn't long enough."

Knox ignored her. He had reached the far corner of the house by the time the police dispatcher acknowledged the call.

Michelle headed cautiously for the front door, head low, gun drawn. Knox opened it as she got there. He had entered through the back door, which had been left ajar.

Helen Stern was the only person in the house.

Michelle, Knox, and I waited in the library for Matthews and the medical examiner.

In another five minutes, the house was full. I sat in the mustard chair, staring at book spines, staying out of the way until Matthews came in to talk. I wished I could be waiting for Helen Stern instead. I mourned her loss, wishing I had known her better. Wishing, too, that someone else had found her body.

"She was shot in the right temple at close range," Matthews said, leaning his bulk against a bookcase on the other side of the small table. "If I had to make a judgment right now, I'd say the perp planned to fake a suicide. You fouled it up."

"Lucky me. When I got here there was an open file drawer. Anything missing?"

"We don't know. That'll take a while. What about you?"

I knew he wasn't asking about my emotional state.

"I wanted Darla Hayden's new address. I wasn't sure you'd give it to me."

"You're right, I wouldn't have. But what you don't know is that Darla Hayden gave her old address when she was booked. It was on her driver's license, so nobody questioned it. We don't have her new address either. The perp may have left it behind, but I wouldn't count on it. Got any other ideas where to get it?"

"Not one." I wasn't lying—I had two or three.

"I don't suppose you know a next of kin or anything."

"Fortunately, I don't."

"Okay. You don't have to stick around now. But I'll need a formal statement."

"Tomorrow. I'll give you a call in the morning."

Matthews went back to the crime scene. I walked outside into the twilight. My hands were shaking, and I didn't feel like driving home. I kept walking.

My original plan for dinner had been to meet Deke at the Mother Lode. I decided there was no reason to change it. I wavered for an instant as I walked past Curtis's apartment building, but I made it to the park, and across the Truckee. Then Second Street, then Virginia. By the time I saw flashing neon, I had regained control.

I stepped through the air curtain into the casino and felt

embraced by a clatter of slots, the buzzing of jackpots, all the sounds of the pot of pyrite at the end of the rainbow.

Diane waved to me as I entered the coffee shop. Deke wasn't there.

I sat down at the end of the counter.

"He's so nice-looking," she gushed. "Next time, come early, so I have a chance to say hello before the place fills up."

"Curtis? Yeah, he is." That had been Tuesday night, and this was only Thursday. I felt caught in a time warp, where everything was moving too swiftly around me. "And I'm sure he'd like to say hello to you, too."

"Are you okay? You look a little green around the gills."

"I had kind of a tough day. This is turning into one of those cases."

She wrinkled her forehead in sympathy. "Want a beer?"

I nodded and reached for a Keno ticket. Filling it out didn't feel good. Sitting there alone didn't feel good. When Diane brought the beer, it didn't taste good.

I caught myself wishing that I had stopped to see Curtis.

By the time Deke plonked his heavy body on the stool next to mine, I was drinking a second beer and wallowing in self-pity. Three losing Keno games hadn't made me feel better. They hadn't even distracted me, though, which made me wonder why I was playing.

"Helen Stern got shot. I walked in while the perp was going through her files," I said.

"Hello to you, too," he answered. The two fingers he

held up would shortly produce a beer for him and one more for me.

"Sorry. It's been a rough couple of days."

"At least you didn't get shot. Don't tell me you already fought with that Curtis fellow."

Deke was turned away from me, leaning his hammy forearms on the counter. He had delivered the line without inflection. I couldn't check his eyes to see what he meant. What he wanted.

"Well, actually, Curtis is about the only thing that hasn't gone wrong. In other news, Al had a heart attack, and Ramona stayed with me last night."

"Al gonna be okay?" Deke shifted to face me, and the concern was genuine.

"Yeah. He'll be in the hospital a while, and I don't know how long Ramona plans to be my houseguest, but we'll all three survive."

"Be good for you two to spend some time together, except not when you're going in opposite directions, like you are now."

"We always are, Deke. It's *deja vu* all over again."

"Yogi Berra said that about a ballgame, not somebody's mother."

"He didn't know mine. I really hoped Helen Stern could make a difference. Shit."

"You were going to talk to the shrink about your mother?" His red-rimmed eyes narrowed, as if he were suspicious of my motives.

"I was thinking about it. But it doesn't matter anyway." I took a gulp of beer and wondered where my hamburger was.

"No, but you might think about it again sometime." When I ignored that, he added, "Did you see whomever going through the files?"

"I saw an open file drawer. The nearest I got to whomever was a bullet above my head."

"You think it could have been your employer?"

"I haven't thought about it."

I wasn't very hungry, though, when Diane put a hamburger in front of me and a steak in front of Deke.

"Maybe you haven't wanted to think about it, but you better." Deke slashed a hunk off his steak and put it in his mouth.

I toyed with the fries.

"It has to have something to do with where she moved."

"Why? Maybe the killer was just afraid of something in the notes, something Darla might have said about him."

"Or her," I said. "I'm not counting out either Jeannie Hiller or Brianne McKinley at this point."

"Then why the address?"

"Because she gave her old one to the police. After not leaving a forwarding address with the post office or anywhere else, including the Mother Lode, when she must have needed that check." I smeared mustard on the hamburger bun, put it all together with the lettuce and tomato slice, and took a bite. It tasted better than I expected.

"But the shrink had it?"

I nodded until I swallowed. "And now I have to find someone else who has it."

"And be careful asking, too."

"Yeah, I will. But we're both assuming Helen Stern was killed because of Darla Hayden. For all either of us knows, a deranged former patient decided to get even for sins real or imagined."

Deke shook his head. "Could be, but don't count on it. Count on somebody having the address and a gun. You want company, let me know."

"Thanks. I will."

I didn't want to bring up Curtis, I didn't want to talk about Ramona, and I didn't really have anything more to say about the case. But one of the strengths of long-standing friendships is toleration of silence. And that was pretty much how we spent the rest of dinner.

Deke didn't even comment when I told the Keno runner that I was through playing for the evening.

When Deke and I parted company at the foot of the escalator, I had to decide whether I was going to walk back to Helen Stern's house and pick up the Jeep or walk straight home, which was only slightly farther. Picking up the Jeep meant passing Curtis's building again, and I knew I didn't have the will to keep from ringing the buzzer a second time.

The evening was a little too cool for walking comfortably in a denim jacket, but I made it home.

Sitting in my cracked leather chair, in my quiet office, was soothing. Until I thought of Helen Stern, alone in her office when the murderer entered. I got up and checked the house, making certain doors and windows were secure.

There were seven messages on my machine. Ramona

would be spending the night at Lake Tahoe. Sandra and Don were looking forward to dinner tomorrow—seven o'clock, at a restaurant near the golf course. Curtis said he was going out to eat, but to call him when I could. Mark Martin wanted to know if I'd make a statement for the eleven o'clock news. So did three reporters I didn't know.

Curtis was still out. His machine answered. I could have picked up my car after all, ringing his buzzer or not. I didn't bother calling any of the others.

Butch and Sundance began chasing each other up and down the hall, a signal that they hadn't been fed since morning. I was almost too tired to respond.

I dragged myself to the kitchen and split a can between the two dishes that Ramona had used. The paper towels beneath them were already spotted with food. One of the cats had ripped a corner off, annoyed that I was late.

The triangle of paper stuck to my boot. I peeled it off and dropped it into the fresh trash bag that Ramona had lined the garbage pail with.

I was so emotionally worn that I didn't even feel guilty for being glad she wasn't there.

I crawled into bed and started flicking through the channels. I stopped when I saw John Wayne riding through the desert with Jeffrey Hunter following him. I remembered in time how annoyed I get when he tries to shoot Natalie Wood, after presumably searching for her all those years to bring her home. I clicked the remote a few more times. I was watching a car chase from a movie I couldn't identify and thinking about turning off the set, wondering if I could fall asleep, when the phone rang.

"I'm sorry I missed your call," Curtis said. "I had dinner with Horton Robb, and I just got home."

"Did you hear about Helen Stern?"

"The report came in over the City News Wire right before we left. It mentioned you. That was why I tried to get in touch. Are you all right?"

"Yeah. I think so, anyway. I'm too tired to be certain. What did the report say?"

"That she had been found dead in her office and you had called the police. I gathered you found her."

"Yeah. And almost the guy who murdered her. My timing was a little off."

"Did you see anything that would put you in danger?"

"No. Whoever it was had to be an amateur—he shot high through a closed door."

Curtis was silent for so long I was afraid he hadn't heard me.

"I didn't know someone shot at you." His voice was low and quiet. "You may be used to this, but I'm not. I'd feel better if you weren't alone tonight. Is your mother there?"

"No, she's gone home to get fresh clothes." I struggled with what he said about being alone, trying to figure out who would be meeting whose needs if he came over. "And I'm fine alone. Really. In fact, I'm too tired to cope with anybody else right now."

"You're sure?"

"Yeah." I hoped he understood. I was almost too tired to care if he didn't. "I like knowing you're there, though."

"There, signifying a distance you want to maintain."

"Come on. Don't play word games with me. I'll be on

campus tomorrow, and if I miss you, I'll come to your place at six-thirty. Sandra and Don want to meet us at seven for dinner, if that's all right with you."

He was silent again. I shut my eyes and waited.

"Well—if you're sure that's what you want. I'll see you tomorrow."

"Thanks."

"By the way—" he caught me just before I said good-bye—"you might want to watch the news, if you can stay awake that long. Darla Hayden's sister, Sharon Turner, read a prepared statement for the cameras."

"What?" I was alert again. "Nobody told me she was in town."

"The police only found her yesterday. She flew up from Sacramento last night."

"Oh, hell. Thanks for letting me know."

"You're welcome. Call me if you change your mind about company."

I promised, knowing I wouldn't change my mind. Butch was stretched out along my legs, one paw on my foot. Sundance was curled up next to my hip. Reason enough not to move.

I flicked channels until I found something medical with enough quick camera cuts and fake blood to keep me from dozing off before Brianne McKinley and Lane Josten could welcome me to the news.

Film clips of the university showed Rick Rodriguez cut off by the siren. Some administrator talked about the need for restraint, the need for life to go on even in the wake of tragedy, and all that. Then Sharon Turner, an older, saner version of her dead sister, read her statement from the steps of the courthouse. The excerpt shown was a call for Aaron Hiller's arrest, almost an echo of what Rick Rodriguez had said. She said letters from her sister described him as a violent man. Roger Wade maintained his client hadn't been arrested because his client was innocent. Mark Martin reported live on Helen Stern's murder, standing outside her dark house. Fortunately, he didn't mention that I'd been there. The district attorney, when asked if the two murders were connected, said that was a possibility.

Lane Josten, smiling as if he hadn't been watching, promised that sports were coming up next. Brianne looked down at her notes, unsmiling for once.

I couldn't make it through the first commercial, the woman telling me which toothpaste her father, a dentist, wanted her to use. I imagined John Wayne as the dentist. Brush your teeth, Natalie, or he'll shoot. I flicked off the set.

I hoped Aaron had an alibi for the time when Helen Stern was murdered. I suspected he would have at least two, whether he needed them or not.

The telephone rang, but I let the machine pick it up. Just in case my name had cropped up on one of the other stations, I pulled the plug on the bedroom phone. I didn't want to talk to reporters, and anyone else could wait until morning.

I dreamed about being chased by ringing phones in the night. But when I checked in the morning, there were only two messages on the machine, both from reporters.

I had stayed in bed as long as I could, thinking about Helen Stern. She was sitting so quietly behind her desk when I walked in. The shot had to have been unexpected, no time for her even to feel threatened. So the shot had to have come from a gun held by someone she had agreed to talk with. I wondered if that let Aaron off the hook.

I got up when I became too restless to lie there. I started to feel guilty about Ramona when I checked the machine. She couldn't have reached me even in an emergency. I tried to get her at the lake. I hung up as her machine clicked on. I could try her later at the hospital. I could even stop by when I was finished at the university.

I left a message on Sandra's home machine, confirming dinner at seven.

Even rested, I didn't feel like going back into the fray. I was actually glad I had to walk over to Court Street to pick up my Jeep.

Standing on the front porch, warmed by the September sun, I had to decide whether my statement to Matthews came first or last in priority for the day. I wanted to make it last. I turned north toward the police station anyway. I had to find out if anything Sharon Turner told them had strengthened their case against Aaron.

Danny Sinclair, the officer at the desk, was on the phone, but he was obviously expecting me. He pointed down the hall toward the detectives' room.

Matthews was on the phone, too. He pointed at the chair next to his desk and handed me a clipboard with Michelle Urrutia's report on it. I listened while I read, hoping he'd say something useful. His grunts didn't convey much.

When he hung up, he leaned on his elbow and waited.

"This is it," I said. "Nothing new since yesterday."

"You told Urrutia you didn't touch anything. That true?"

"Yeah. Why?"

"Just wanted to make sure."

I didn't believe him. "What did you find?"

"A brass tiger." He watched me to see if I intended to react. I didn't. "Inscribed to Aaron Hiller from some guy with a long Japanese name. There was dried blood on it, along with some very smeared fingerprints. I checked it with the medical examiner. He thinks it could be the murder weapon used to kill Hayden."

"The answer is, not only did I not take it there, I didn't even notice it, either in Aaron's office or in Helen Stern's."

"It's okay, I believe you. Don't get defensive with me. You want some coffee?" He kept leaning on his elbow as if he didn't really want to get it.

"No, thanks." I didn't think I'd been defensive. "If somebody was trying to fake a suicide, maybe somebody was trying to frame Helen Stern for Darla Hayden's murder, too."

"Yeah, that was what I figured. But with Aaron Hiller the only serious suspect, who had something to gain by the frame?"

"Oh, hell, Matthews. What you're heading toward is that Aaron could have murdered Darla, left her lying in his office in his panic—but took the murder weapon with him—then tried to shift the blame to Helen Stern with a faked suicide. Right?" The growing knot in my stomach argued that I was heading toward the same conclusion.

"It's possible, O'Neal. Either Hiller or somebody hired by Hiller."

"Quit looking at me like that. I'm the one who got shot at yesterday, remember?"

"Yeah. You're not a suspect. I think you genuinely liked Stern. And I don't think you could live with helping a murderer stay free. You're also the one contact I got in the Hiller camp. Whatever you hear, I want to know about it."

"I'll do what I can. But I'd have to report it to Roger Wade first."

Matthews nodded as solemnly as an altar boy. "Of course. You sure you don't have anything for me now?"

"Nothing's happened since yesterday. Except I heard Sharon Turner's statement on television last night. And I'd still like to have Darla Hayden's most recent address."

"So would we. The sister didn't know she'd moved. Hadn't heard from her in months."

"Then what was she saying about letters?"

"All old ones, and not much help." He sighed as if the hope had gone out of his chest. "A couple of references to Hiller's temper, that's all. No threats."

"Okay. I'll stay in touch." I stood and held out my hand.

Matthews looked up at me with hound dog eyes, taking my hand with the paw he wasn't leaning on. "That's all I'm asking."

I retraced my steps along the yellow line, slipped past Danny Sinclair, and walked out into the sunshine.

At least I knew what Rick Rodriguez was talking

about when he said something was missing from Aaron's office. The next thing was to make sure that his sister had told him. And find out the new address.

Asking Aaron about the tiger was on the list, but I figured he'd plead ignorance of its loss.

I started west on Second, trying to think of a way to get to my car without passing Curtis's building. There wasn't a good one. I didn't stop only because I assured myself he wasn't there. He'd be either at the television station or the university.

I got in the Jeep and headed north.

I had almost reached the campus when I changed my mind and turned west on University Terrace. I could bet Aaron Hiller hadn't gone to his office, but he might be at home. It was past time for him to give me some answers on what had happened that night with Darla Hayden.

The blue Ford Taurus was in the driveway. This time, a dark green Lexus was parked beside it. I pulled in at an angle that blocked both cars.

Jeannie Hiller met me on the front porch. She was wearing a frayed terrycloth robe, and her eyes were damp and frantic.

"Thank goodness you're here." She clutched at my shoulder. "I tried to call you, and Roger's on his way."

"What's going on?"

"Aaron's locked himself in his office, with a gun. He says he's going to kill himself."

# Chapter
## 13

"AARON? IT'S FREDDIE O'Neal." I stood in the hall and knocked on his office door, feeling like a total idiot. What the hell could I say to him?

Jeannie Hiller hovered behind me in the archway that led from the living room. One hand was against her throat, as if she might be getting ready for the mad scene from *Lucia di Lammermoor*.

I prayed Roger Wade was hotfooting it over.

"Aaron?" I knocked again. "I need to know what's going on." I waited as long as I could for an answer. "Aaron, I don't have a lot of choices here. Your wife told me you have a gun. I can't keep standing here and waiting for the sound of a bullet. This is a simple lock, and I can force it with a credit card so that we can talk. Or I can call the police. I'll give you a ten count to decide. One, two . . ." I spaced the numbers, but I still got to eight.

"I don't want the police."

I could hardly hear the words. I had pulled out a credit card, in case he agreed, and I opened the door before he could change his mind. I stepped through and left it slightly ajar, hoping to encourage anyone who wanted to interrupt.

Aaron Hiller was sitting in a chair behind a smooth, dark desk, clear except for a personal computer, staring into a far corner. He didn't look up as I entered.

I couldn't see much of the room, because the closed venetian blinds covering the window behind him were only admitting slivers of light. From what I could tell, the Japanese motif had only been extended to the wall hangings between the bookcases and one flowered futon on a bamboo frame. There weren't any tatami mats for me to tear up with my boots.

I eased myself onto the futon, forearms on my knees.

The gun was dangling from his right hand. If he started to bring it up, I could probably get to it before he fired. Probably. And if you shoot a pair of dice, seven will probably come up. But it doesn't necessarily happen on the first roll.

"What are you doing here?" His voice was still low and growly, and he still hadn't looked at me.

"I came to get answers to some questions. That gun in your hand has just added a couple more to the list. You might think about putting it down."

I wished Helen Stern were there talking to him.

I wished Helen Stern were alive.

"If I were any kind of a man, I would have used it." His hand tensed on the gun, then relaxed again. "I'll never recover from this. My reputation has been shattered, my honor along with it."

"Reputation, maybe. Why honor? If you've told the truth, why is your honor gone?"

Aaron glanced at me, shook his head, and focused again on the corner.

"Darla Hayden died because of me. How can I atone for that except by my own death?"

"You mean you did kill her?"

If there were any justice in the universe, someone would be listening.

"No, he didn't kill her, I did!" *Lucia di Lammermoor* flung open the door. Not quite what I had prayed for.

"Get out of here!" Aaron shouted. He whipped the gun up and around, pointing it at Jeannie, too fast for me to react. "Get the hell out of here!"

"Jeannie, go!" I echoed.

She wavered, swinging on the door.

"But I killed her," she whimpered.

"Then call the police," I snapped. "Now! That's the honorable way to end this."

Aaron turned to me, gun still pointed at Jeannie.

"Don't talk glibly of honor."

I saw his eyes for the first time. And I believed he could fire the gun. At somebody.

"If that's glib, explain it to me," I said. "What's honorable about suicide? What's honorable about threatening your wife?"

He looked down at his hand, then brought the gun up, leaning his forehead against it. "I shouldn't have threatened my wife."

"What else shouldn't you have done?"

"Nothing! He didn't do it!" Jeannie shrieked.

Aaron didn't react. Jeannie clung to the door, staring at him in terror.

"Jeannie, why don't you see what's keeping Roger?" I had balled my hands into fists, wishing I could strike out at one of them.

"Roger," she said, not moving. "That's right, I called Roger."

"Would you rather talk to Roger?" I asked. When he didn't answer, I added, "There can't be much honor in blowing your brains out in front of your wife."

"No, I suppose not," he said. "Perhaps we should sit here quietly until Roger arrives."

Time froze. Aaron sat with the gun near his head, not quite poised to shoot. Jeannie slipped to the floor, breathing in deep gasps. I stayed on the futon, still prepared to rush him if I had to. Finally, we heard a car stop in front. The car door slammed, then footsteps raced to the door I had left open when Jeannie let me in.

"Aaron? Jeannie?" Roger shouted.

In a moment, he was towering over Jeannie in the entrance to the room. He lurched to a stop when he saw the gun in Aaron's hand.

"Oh, hell. Aaron. Please, put the gun down," he said.

Aaron looked up at him. "There's no honorable way out of this."

"Goddamn it, Aaron, you don't live in Japan!"

Somehow Roger's terror was easing my own. I grabbed the bamboo futon frame and pulled myself to my feet.

"You really need a sword for hara-kiri," I said.

"Shut up!" Roger screamed.

"Hell. She's right. I don't know what I think I'm

doing." Aaron put the gun on the desk and began to sob.

I lunged for the gun as Jeannie threw herself across the desk.

"Oh, baby, baby," she cried, covering Aaron with her body.

"I'll take the gun," Roger said, holding out his hand.

"I don't think so. If this is the gun that was used to murder Helen Stern, then it has to be turned over to the police," I answered.

I wasn't afraid of him, but I backed to a safe distance. I also didn't want to have to threaten him with the gun.

"Helen Stern?" Aaron's voice was muffled by his wife's shoulder. "Why would someone shoot Helen Stern with my gun?"

"She was shot with somebody's gun. A brass tiger with your name on it—which might have been the weapon used to bludgeon Darla Hayden—was found in Helen's office. The police think the murderer might have been trying to fake her suicide and frame her for Darla's death. Since you're the prime suspect in one killing, you're automatically a suspect in the second one."

Aaron tried to disentangle himself and stand up, but Jeannie screamed when he pulled at her arm.

"It's all right." He patted her clumsily on the back. "I promise. It's all right now. We'll all move to the living room. You could fix tea for our guests."

She slowly released her grip and slid off the desk, almost landing on the floor again. Roger caught her.

"I don't need tea," he said.

"Thank you. But I'd like to fix tea." Jeannie held on to Roger's arm until she could control her breath. She couldn't quite manage to smile at him before she started stiffly out of the room.

Aaron looked from Roger to me, as if expecting us to go with her.

"If you don't mind, I'll bring up the rear," I said.

He nodded. I waited until both men were in the hall, then followed a respectful three paces behind. I still had the gun.

Aaron and Roger both settled onto the futon behind the low table with the chrysanthemums. I sank onto the one at right angles, where I had been sitting the day before, and placed the gun between my feet.

"The brass tiger was a gift from the late Senator Hayakawa, in recognition for my cross-cultural efforts," Aaron said. "I didn't realize at first that it was missing."

"Why didn't you say something when you *did* realize?" I asked.

"We discussed telling the police," Roger said. "I felt there might be a good tactical moment and advised Aaron to wait."

"Making tactical decisions on what and when to tell the police is your choice." I hoped they heard the disapproval in my tone. "But if you want me to stay involved, you have to keep me informed. So before your wife comes back, I want to know—were you the person Darla Hayden engaged in consensual intercourse with shortly before she was murdered?"

The two men looked at each other. Roger shrugged his shoulders.

"If you don't want to answer," I added, "I'll just submit a report saying that Jeannie's confession provides another viable suspect. Therefore I've done my job and I quit."

"Jeannie's confession?" Roger straightened as best he could from his cramped position on the futon. His legs were longer than mine. He had to be uncomfortable.

"She didn't mean it." Aaron turned from Roger to me. "You know that. She was hysterical. She thought she was protecting me."

"In other words, she didn't kill Darla Hayden, but she thinks you might have. Is that it?"

"I don't know what she thinks, Freddie. We haven't really confronted what happened that night." He dropped his voice to a level of intimacy that didn't seem quite appropriate. "And the truth is—as you and the police suspect—that I did have consensual intercourse with Darla Hayden in my office. I'm embarrassed to admit it, even to you, and I hope the murderer is found before I have to discuss it publicly. Because I didn't kill her. I swear it." He raised his right hand like a Boy Scout.

"How did it happen?" I asked.

"God, I don't know. When she got out of jail on Saturday, she sent me an E-mail message asking me to meet her on campus the next evening. She said she had decided to file a lawsuit against the university, and she wanted to let me know about it. I hoped I could talk her out of it. I didn't intend to touch her." He leaned forward, pleading with me to sympathize. "Darla—God, there was something so erotic about her, every time I saw her. And it was still there—a magnetic field that I walked into, and I didn't know how to get out of it without discharging. She felt it as well. She always did."

"Sure she did. She even wanted you to hit her, right?"

The sympathetic Aaron fell to the angry one. "She goaded me! No one, no one understands how she goaded me. I did hit her! But I didn't kill her!"

"Okay. I believe you. So was she going to drop the lawsuit?"

"I don't even know that. I left her rather abruptly, I'm afraid." He buried his face in his hands.

"In your office?"

"You know, Aaron isn't on trial—" Roger began. But he was too late. Aaron had already nodded. He had lied about that, at least. He hadn't left Darla Hayden at the front door of the building. He had left her in his office. After fucking her on his couch.

I wanted the son of a bitch to be guilty so much that my stomach knotted. But I believed he hadn't killed her.

"I'm sorry—I'm afraid this was all I could come up with. I wasn't expecting guests." Jeannie Hiller placed a bamboo tray with a teapot, four cups, napkins, and a plate of raw veggies, cheese cubes, and crackers on the table. She sat cross-legged on a mat and started pouring.

"This is fine, thank you." I took a cup from her hand.

Roger did the same. When Aaron didn't look up, she carefully placed a cup in front of him.

"Please help yourselves to the food," she said.

Roger compulsively piled three cheese cubes onto a cracker and popped it all in his mouth. I picked up a carrot stick, then put it down on a napkin.

"Jeannie, I don't believe your murder confession. I don't believe Aaron killed Darla Hayden, either. But I'd like to know if you went to the university that evening."

Her face twisted and her shoulders hunched, as if she were curling into a shell.

"I didn't stay. The door was closed, and I couldn't hear what they were saying. I didn't stay." The words came out between guttural sobs.

Roger Wade emptied his teacup.

"Are you still on the job?" he asked.

"Hell. Oh, hell. I guess so. As long as everybody is straight with me."

Nobody even looked at me.

"Can either of you remember seeing anyone else?" I asked.

Nobody moved.

"This may not be the right time to ask," Roger said.

"Well, then, when is?" I snapped. "Is there a tactical moment to ask about murder?"

"I didn't see anyone," Jeannie whispered.

Aaron shook his head.

I wanted to leave, but I wasn't certain my knees would hold if I tried to stand. And there wouldn't be a better tactical moment.

"Did Darla give you her new address?" I asked.

"No." Aaron lifted his head. "She offered it, but I told her no."

"Did she say anything that might help me find it?"

"I'll have to think. She said something about being with people who cared about her." His brow furrowed.

"Did she mention names?"

"Names? I don't think so." Aaron looked at the three of us, as if someone might leap in.

Nobody did.

I put down the teacup and picked up the gun.

"What are you doing?" Roger asked.

"Leaving."

"Not with the gun," he said.

"Fuck you. I'm not returning a gun to a man who waved it at his wife and held it against his own forehead." My knees didn't buckle when I stood up. "Let me know if you make a tactical decision to tell the police about it."

"Profanity isn't necessary. And since I'm sure Jeannie doesn't want to press charges, there's nothing to report to the police." Roger's face was mottled.

Jeannie sat with her head down, hugging herself.

"If that's how you see it." I needed to think about what Matthews ought to know and whether I could tell him. "I'll give you a call when I find another suspect."

Nobody said good-bye as I walked out the door.

I made it to the Jeep and locked the gun in the glove compartment before I started to shake.

When I was certain I could drive, I backed out of the driveway and rolled down the hill.

I didn't feel much like talking to Randy Thurman or Gabriela Rodriguez. In fact, I felt like calling it a day and going home. If I had been certain Ramona wouldn't be there, I might have done it. But I took University Terrace to the campus instead.

Without the news vans and the reporters, the grounds seemed vacant. The parking lot was less than half-full, and there were only a half-dozen students on the path to the student union. Of course, it was Friday afternoon. Not too many classes on Friday afternoon.

The halls of the business school were empty, and most of the office doors were closed.

The finance door was open, but a young woman I hadn't seen before was sitting at Gabriela's desk.

"Could I help you?" she asked.

"Where's Gabriela?"

"She doesn't work on Friday afternoons. I fill in."

Afternoon. That was why I was starting to feel weak. I hadn't had so much as a carrot stick all day.

"We use inexpensive student help whenever possible, to stretch the budget a bit. There's never enough money for everything. Student help is sometimes a good thing. Gabriela called in sick this morning." Randy Thurman was standing in the doorway to his office. He didn't look any better than he had the day before. "Come on in."

He shut the door behind me and waited until we were both settled before he said anything more.

"How do you think I can help Aaron?" He folded his long fingers across his nose. Wide, pale eyes peered at me through round glasses.

"By helping me find out who else was here last Sunday night. Can you check computer log-ons? And how about asking maintenance and security personnel?"

"I could check computer accounts for usage, but that wouldn't tell you whether people were here or in the library or dialing in on modems." He made a note on a deskpad, then looked back up. "There's no maintenance on Sunday night, and not much in the way of security. The campus police have already stated that they didn't see anything unusual."

"But we probably aren't looking for anything unusual.

That's just it. Roger Wade has asked me to find another suspect, somebody besides Aaron who had motive and opportunity. The killer probably knew her—either a professor or another student. Wade doesn't think this was random violence. Neither does Detective Matthews. Do you?"

"Oh, God. I don't know." He gripped the pencil with both hands.

"What about the professor she complained about in her memos? Gary Metzger, I think his name is."

"He's on sabbatical this fall. He isn't even in town."

"Who might have been around?"

Thurman just shook his head.

"Okay. Another thing. Do you have her new address?"

"What?" The pale eyes lost focus.

"Darla Hayden moved not long before she was murdered. If I could find out where, that might help."

"That's right. You were looking for her new address when you first came here. No. No, she didn't give it to the department. Although I suppose we would have had it once she sued." He attempted a smile, but gave it up quickly.

"You knew she was going to sue?"

"Aaron told me on Monday." He shook his head. "This is all so terrible. Who would have thought she'd be so hard and unforgiving?"

"Yeah. Who would have thought her life was more important to her than her career?"

"Exactly. " He seemed pleased that I got it. "Is there anything else you need to know?"

"Not right now. I'll stop by again on Monday for the

computer information." The mention of Aaron had tapped my emotional reserves. I couldn't tell Thurman about the suicide attempt, but I'd have to vent on somebody soon. I also had to do something about the gun in my glove compartment.

Thurman walked me to the door.

"I'll have one of the computer operators check the accounts before Monday. I suppose telling you to have a nice weekend would be inappropriate."

"I think so. But thanks for trying."

I was sorry Gabriela Rodriguez hadn't been there, but I could talk to her Monday as well.

Once in the Jeep, I was again faced with the choice of whether to stop by the hospital or go home.

I had to get food before I did anything else, and when the grease from the drive-thru hamburger dripped onto my jeans, the decision was made. I drove home.

Butch and Sundance were both waiting on the porch. That meant Ramona wasn't inside. One small thing—one large thing—had just gone right in my day.

I moved Aaron's gun from the glove compartment to my desk drawer. I was going to have to do something with it, but I wasn't sure what.

I dragged myself to the bedroom, got out of my sticky jeans, and sat down on the bed. Butch hopped up beside me, purring while Sundance sniffed the hamburger stain. I had to call the hospital, at least that.

Ramona answered when I asked for Al's room.

"How's Al?"

"Resting comfortably," she whispered. "The doctor says that the likelihood of another heart attack is low enough that I don't have to be here all the time unless I want to be. I told him I want to be."

"I understand." My heart was sinking as I said it.

"No, no, I'm not moving in with you. I've taken a room at the Sands, at least for the next few days. They won't care what time I get in, and they'll bring me coffee in bed. Good coffee, not microwaved."

I knew she heard my sigh of relief.

"I really don't want to be in your way," she said. "And between your relationship with Curtis and that murder case, you have your hands full right now."

"Are you sure you're okay alone?" I asked. My eyes were squeezed shut and my fingers crossed.

"I won't exactly be alone. I can take the elevator down to the casino if I get scared, day or night."

"Oh, God, I hope that's a joke."

"It is. What's wrong?"

"I'm just tired. You're right, I have my hands full. But I'll check back with you later. And call me if you want to. You're not in my way." I really tried to mean it.

"Take a nap. Al's stirring, and I don't want to stay on the phone. Say hello to Curtis."

I hung up the phone, pulled the bedcovers to my chin, and shut my eyes. Butch sat on my hip, a furry weight, still purring.

When I opened my eyes again, a bluish gray light filled the room. The clock said six-thirty. I tried to remember what was significant about the time. I tried to figure out if it was dawn or dusk.

I thought back to getting up in the morning and reconstructed the day, as best I could. Matthews. Aaron.

Randy Thurman. Ramona. Who had told me to say hello to Curtis.

Who was expecting me at six-thirty.

I picked up the phone.

"I can't make it," I said when he answered. "I'll call Sandra and tell her we have to reschedule."

"What happened?"

"It involves Aaron Hiller, and I'd tell you if you were an outsider. But he's your colleague, and this is too heavy. I need some time to digest it. Besides, I'm starting to feel that everyone connected with the murder has been saying too much to too many people."

"You sound terrible."

"Yeah, probably. And I can't make polite conversation for two hours, worrying about how you and Sandra are going to get along. I just can't."

"Okay. We'll reschedule. What are you going to do instead?"

"I don't know. Normally, I'd either order a pizza and watch a movie or go look for Deke."

Curtis was silent for a moment. "If you could handle a companion who doesn't require polite conversation, I deliver. But I could understand if you decide you really need to talk to Deke."

I had to think about that. I knew he would try to understand, but breaking the date because I had a bad day I didn't want to tell him about—and then telling Deke about it—called for a lot of understanding.

"Okay, but nothing weird," I said. "Pepperoni and extra cheese."

"No anchovies," he promised.

Sandra offered a little less understanding.

"Why can't you tell me what happened? How can you expect me to say it's okay to break a dinner date when you won't tell me?"

"You're my friend. You have to trust that I had a work-related bad day and let me off the hook for dinner. I'll tell you when I can, and this isn't the night for it." I was just alert enough not to remind her that she was a reporter. "Lunch. We'll do lunch. And we'll reschedule dinner after this is over."

She reluctantly agreed. I almost wished I had lied to her. She would have accepted an emergency with Ramona as an excuse, and it wouldn't have been too far off.

Curtis arrived about half an hour later with a large pizza, a salad, and a six-pack. We spread it all out on the coffee table in front of my sagging couch.

Sundance was right there with his nose in everything. Butch watched from a distance, undecided whether to mooch pepperoni or pout.

"Are you sure you don't want to talk about Aaron?" Curtis asked.

"I don't want to right now. Except to say that I think he's innocent of Darla Hayden's murder. He was distraught today, and I don't think he was putting on an act." That sounded all right.

"Okay. But since neither one of us is thinking about anything other than Aaron, we'd better pick a movie."

It was a sensible suggestion, letting somebody else make conversation for us. He'd even brought videotapes. I'd seen them all, and *Howard's End* was the only one I thought I could make it through again. I would have been more comfortable with Randolph Scott and the cavalry.

And we had to watch the Channel 12 News at Eleven. The only reference to either murder was one more sound bite from Roger Wade, predicting that there would be a breakthrough soon, one that would prove Aaron Hiller was telling the truth.

Curtis and I still didn't have much to say when we went to bed. All in all, it wasn't one of our better nights.

# Chapter
# 14

SATURDAY MORNING WASN'T much of an improvement. Curtis grouched about microwaved coffee, and I grouched back, but we went out for brunch anyway. The meal was awkward, because I still didn't want to discuss Aaron's gun-waving, and I still wasn't up for polite conversation. Fortunately, Curtis was playing tennis at one with Horton Robb.

I went home, turned on the computer, and pulled up Tetris. I know some people think games are time-wasters. For me, watching the blocks fall drains off tension. I was having trouble focusing on the case without dissolving into fury at Aaron Hiller's self-absorption. I had to come at this from a different angle, so I could replay in my head what I had seen and heard the day before without being part of it.

There had be a next step I could take to find where Darla Hayden had been living. She had told Aaron she was with people who cared about her. But the person who had bailed her out of jail—Helen Stern—was dead. Her sister hadn't heard from her.

And the only concern I had seen on campus had been written on signs.

If the people who cared about her, the ones who took her in, were the other graduate students, that might explain why she had suddenly decided to sue.

I turned off the computer and picked up a telephone directory. In the half-column of Rodriguezes, a *G* and an *R* were listed at the same address on Cheney Street, in an area of crumpling cheap apartment buildings and ramshackle frame houses that could shelter a cluster of graduate students. And it wasn't far.

The drive was less than ten minutes. I parked the Jeep in front of a two-story house badly in need of paint. The wide porch was a sign that it had probably been built more than fifty years ago. And nobody had bothered to water the lawn since. One old locust tree was thriving on annual rainfall, thanks to a root system wide enough to tap a neighbor's largess and strong enough to crack the sidewalk.

I avoided the cracks and rang the doorbell.

"Oh, hell," Rick Rodriguez said when he opened the door. He barely swung it wide enough for me to wedge a boot tip in.

"Who is it?" a woman's voice asked.

"Your friend. The one who works for Aaron Hiller."

Gabriela ducked under his arm.

"Hi, Freddie. Come on in."

She ducked back inside. Rick reluctantly let me pass.

The living room looked like a students' lounge. The sofa was covered by a fringed Indian blanket. The four chairs were old, unmatched, and shredded by what might have been generations of cats. A Frida Kahlo poster was tacked to one wall, and a cheap reproduction of a Charles Russell cowboy hung on another. All other decorations were books—stacked on the coffee table, stacked on shelves, stacked on the floor.

The woman who had brought the signs to the demonstration was stretched out on the sofa with an open book. When she saw me, she got up and left the room without a word.

"Have a seat," Gabriela said. "We've talked about you. You want tea or something?"

"No, thanks. What did you say about me?" I sat in a chair that had white tufts sprouting from upholstery that was somewhere between indigo and black.

"I said you were okay. You were doing a job, and we could trust you." Gabriela sat in a dark green chair across from me.

"And you?" I asked Rick.

"Shit." He sat on the arm of the couch and looked down on me. "There are ways to make a living that are wrong. What kind of person takes a job to help a guilty man evade punishment?"

"That's a tough one," I admitted. "And I struggled with it. But I don't think Aaron Hiller is guilty of murder, whatever I may dislike about him. For the record, I'm not sure what I would have done if the evidence had stacked up against him."

"Come on!" Rick leaned forward, a little too close. "He murdered Darla. What do you want?"

"Tell me what you know."

"If it convicts him?"

"If it convicts him, you need to talk to Detective Matthews."

"White male cops don't listen to Mexicans."

"Well, I have to struggle with that one, too."

"He's right," Gabriela said. "You know it."

"No, I don't know it. It isn't that simple." I looked from one to the other. "I think Matthews is a good cop who would listen to you because he cares about what really happened. I think that partly because he listens to me. Tell me what you know, and we'll go from there. Start with why Darla Hayden agreed to move in with you."

"You know that?" Gabriela asked.

I nodded and uncrossed my fingers.

"She was alone too much," Gabriela said. "When they told her she was out of the program, she wandered around the campus like a ghost. That was why I gave copies of her memos to Rick."

She glanced at him, and he picked up the story.

"I saw her one night in the library, sitting at a computer terminal, tears running down her face. I said maybe we should go get a cup of coffee. She was really upset. I had to turn off the terminal and drag her away."

A calico cat rubbed against Rick's leg. He reached down and lifted her onto his knee.

"At first she was angry that I knew about the memos," he continued. "But then she calmed down, and she promised to think about what I said—that we all had problems with the system, although hers were the worst. And if she really wanted revenge, she should expose them. She should let us support her while she sued Aaron Hiller and the university and everybody."

"And she agreed?" I asked.

"Not that night. She called me the next morning, wanting to know if I would help her move. I told her to pack, and I'd be there at midnight with some friends and a truck." He stroked the purring cat without looking at her.

"Darla was still upset when she got here," Gabriela said. "She stayed in bed for two days, with boxes all around her. Rick took her food, and he insisted that we exempt her from house rules about cooperation until she felt better. Even the first night she came downstairs for dinner, she wouldn't talk to anybody."

"But by the next day, it was like she had made some kind of commitment," Rick said. "We made plans for what to do next."

"The scene at the faculty center with the toy gun? You thought that was a good move?"

Rick shook his head. "Darla said that she couldn't sue without giving the university a final opportunity to make things right. So she sent Professor Thurman a memo explaining that she had joined the graduate students' union and she was ready to take action."

"That was the memo I wanted to give you a copy of," Gabriela said. "But I had to check with Rick first. And anyway, it wasn't in the files anymore when I looked."

"Randy Thurman knew Darla was going to file a lawsuit?" I didn't want to hear that.

"Sure. A couple of weeks ago," Rick said. "When he

ignored her memo, she thought up the toy gun scheme to announce it, and I couldn't talk her out of it."

"Why weren't you there to back her up?"

"She wanted to do it alone. I was waiting for her at the library. I didn't know the situation had blown up until I heard the sirens."

"And you didn't want to get involved with the cops," I said.

"I would have if she had asked me to." Rick said it so firmly that I believed him. "But she asked the shrink to bail her out of jail, not me."

"The shrink. Helen Stern. Did you hear about her murder?"

"Yeah. I saw it on the news." Gabriela leaned forward in her chair. "The reporter said somebody shot her and tried to make it look like suicide. I couldn't go back to work after I heard. I've been afraid to leave home."

"Why?"

"Why was she murdered, unless it was because she tried to help Darla Hayden? That means we have to stick together, right? Just like the fat ones stick together."

"I don't understand. Who are the fat ones?"

"The ones with power," Rick explained. "The administrators. The professors. The lawyers. Them."

"What makes you think there was some kind of conspiracy here?"

"Darla went to campus Sunday night to meet Professor Hiller," Rick said. "She was going to discuss the lawsuit with him. She didn't come back. She was murdered in his office. Who else would murder her? He used to beat Darla when he said he loved her. What kind of man would do that? And what would he do when she threatened to go public with the kind of man he was?"

I didn't have an answer.

"Then on Monday, when Darla's body was discovered, I saw Professor Hiller's brass tiger in Professor Thurman's office. He put it there, so the police wouldn't find it. On Tuesday, it was gone entirely. Professor Hiller killed Darla with the brass tiger, and Professor Thurman covered for him." Gabriela's eyes filled. She didn't bother to wipe them.

I had to wipe mine. "I don't think Professor Hiller was aware of how the tiger left his office. Do you know whether Professor Thurman was on campus Sunday night?"

"Professor Thurman?" Gabriela shook her head. "I know he worked on the budget over the weekend, to see how the department could make it through until June, but he could have been working from home."

"Yes. The computer log-on wouldn't show where he was working." As he had reminded me. I wondered if anyone could place Thurman at home. A wife, maybe. I somehow doubted it.

"You think Professor Thurman killed her?" Rick was frowning. That didn't fit with his neat scenario of rage and passion.

"I don't know. I just don't know. But as of right now, I think the circumstantial evidence may point to him."

"Oh, no." Rick bounced off the arm of the sofa, dumping the protesting calico cat to the floor. "What good did it do to talk to you? All you want is to keep

Professor Hiller out of jail. And you'll confuse the issue by pointing to Professor Thurman to do it."

"No, damn it, that isn't what I want to do."

"But it's what you're paid to do, right?" He had made it about three paces away. He whirled to face me. "Aaron Hiller bought you, and you're going to give him what he paid for!"

"I hope you're wrong, I really do." I shouted the last words, but he was out of the room before I had finished the sentence. I stood and held out my hand to Gabriela. "I don't think your trust in me is misplaced. At least I hope not. And I'll stay in touch. In the meantime, maybe you're right to stay away from work and stick close to Rick."

I didn't know whether either of them was in danger. But I still wasn't quite sure why Helen Stern had been murdered. Or by whom. As much as I had wanted Aaron Hiller to be guilty, I wanted Randy Thurman to be innocent.

Gabriela waved good-bye from the porch.

I could have put off calling Roger Wade, I know that. Nevertheless, I had to give him the information about Randy Thurman and the brass tiger. Rick was partly right. Aaron Hiller was paying me, and I owed him something. If some evidence pointing to Thurman was enough, he might not want to pay for anything more.

So I called Roger as soon as I got home and told him the story.

"His secretary said Thurman had the tiger?" Roger didn't seem to quite get it.

"That's right. And while I didn't ask directly, I don't

think she knew the tiger ended up on Helen Stern's desk. She did say she'd heard about the second murder on television. But as far as I'm aware, the tiger wasn't part of the report."

"Maybe the two of them did it."

"What?"

"Well, that makes more sense than Randy Thurman, for Christ's sake. The student radical bashed the girl's head in, and his sister is covering for him by implicating Thurman."

"No. No, Roger, no. That isn't what happened."

"Sure. Whatever. Anyway, you've done your job. I'll let you know if we need anything more, but for now, you can consider yourself off the case."

"What are you going to do now?"

"Give Brianne a call. Ask her for help in getting some positive media spin on this."

Shit.

"By the way," he added, "Aaron wants his gun back."

"Tell him he'll get it next time I see him."

I sat there holding the phone after Roger had hung up. I didn't want Roger hurling accusations at Rick and Gabriela Rodriguez on the evening news. That would not only feed into their conspiracy theory, it would make me part of it, as well. I couldn't stand the thought of making life worse for them.

Roger had said I was off the case. And he hadn't asked me to keep my opinions about Thurman to myself.

I called the police station. Matthews wasn't there, but I persuaded the desk officer that I had important information. He promised to beep Matthews for me.

The phone rang about ten minutes later.

"What have you got for me?" Matthews asked.

"It seems the brass tiger made a stop on Randy Thurman's desk before it got to Helen Stern's," I said. "Did the ME confirm that it was the murder weapon?"

"In a manner of speaking. Hayden had three cracked ribs, one puncturing her lung, and a ruptured spleen. Without a fast trip to the hospital, she would have been dead anyway. The blows to her head just speeded things up."

"Shit."

Darla Hayden was alive when Aaron left her. He had told the truth about that. But she wouldn't have been for long.

"We couldn't get clear fingerprints from the tiger," Matthews said. "How credible is the person you talked to?"

"I believe her. Darla Hayden was living with her." I explained to Matthews how I had discovered Rick and Gabriela Rodriguez. I also told him that Roger Wade was prepared to point a finger toward them on the evening news.

"That scumbag," Matthews said. "Okay. We did lift some unidentified prints from Stern's desk drawer. I'll have them checked against Thurman's."

"I don't suppose you can do anything to stop Wade."

"It's a free country with a free press. If he slanders the Rodriguezes, they can hire a lawyer."

"Sure."

"I gotta go, O'Neal. Thanks for calling. And keep in touch."

I replaced the phone, wondering what I ought to do next. Nothing I did seemed to be improving the situation much. About the best thing happening was that I didn't have to prove Thurman shot Helen Stern. Or prove anybody else did, either.

The afternoon faded to twilight. I was still staring at the phone when the doorbell rang. The cats headed for the hall, so I knew it wasn't Ramona.

Nevertheless, the last person I expected to find on my front porch was Randy Thurman.

"May I come in?"

He looked like an abandoned puppy shivering in a rumpled shirt and sport coat. I couldn't say no.

I didn't want to turn it into a social call, so I gestured toward one of the rickety client chairs and returned to my spot behind the desk.

"Aaron called me," he said, blinking pale eyes behind round glasses. "He said you told Roger Wade that I could be linked to the murders, and even though he didn't believe Roger would do anything with the information, someone else might. I don't understand."

"The brass tiger," I said. "Someone hit Darla Hayden over the head with Aaron's brass tiger. The tiger ended up on Helen Stern's desk, when someone—presumably the same person—shot Helen and tried to make it look like suicide. A witness is willing to testify that the brass tiger was in your office for a period of time between the two murders."

"Gabriela must have seen it there." He smoothed his sparse hair with one long-fingered hand. "Is there some way we can keep this from the police?"

"I'm afraid not. I've already told Detective Matthews." That came out before I thought about it.

"But you worked for Aaron." Randy Thurman shifted in the uncomfortable chair. "You're Curtis Breckinridge's friend. I thought I could trust you. Why would you talk to the detective before you talked to me?"

"Then you don't deny it was there?"

"Well—I suppose it would be my word against Gabriela's, wouldn't it?"

"Unless you left your fingerprints on Helen Stern's desk drawer."

He started blinking again.

"What made you think you could trust me to cover up murder?" I asked.

"I thought you would understand what was really important here—you seemed to care so much about the university. And I didn't mean to kill her. I didn't even mean to hurt her. I've been thinking about discussing it with you, thinking you might help me figure out a way to handle this that would save the reputation of the department. You appear to be not only an intelligent person, but one who is comfortable dealing with criminal matters. I don't know anyone else I can tell." He leaned forward earnestly.

I didn't want to get angry with him. Getting angry wouldn't help. And I did understand what was really important here.

"If you didn't mean to hurt Darla, why did you pick up the tiger?"

"To defend myself." He said it as if it must be obvious. "I was in my office Sunday night, working on the budget, when I heard a woman shouting in the hall. I came out to find Darla Hayden, leaning against the open door to Aaron's office. She was obviously in considerable pain, and I thought I might be able to help her. When she realized who I was, she became hysterical. She grabbed my coat and pulled me into Aaron's office. She said I shouldn't have ignored her memo."

Randy broke off, as if he might have to explain.

"The one in which she let you know she was going to sue the university," I said.

He nodded. "I made a mistake on that. I thought it was just another bid for attention, and reacting to it would only encourage her. I realized when she came to the faculty center with the toy gun that I should have responded, told her that we just didn't have the budgetary resources to defend a lawsuit. Thrown myself on her mercy."

He couldn't smile at his own joke. It took him a moment to continue. "But by Sunday night, it was too late for me to do anything. Aaron had enraged her, and she transferred the rage to me. Not for the first time, I might add. She was going to expose us all, she said, and she had friends who would help her. Then she started screaming, and she grabbed me again."

His hands began fluttering around his head. "I was frantic. I didn't know what to do. And then I made another mistake. I picked up the tiger from Aaron's desk and hit her with it. I just wanted her to let go of me. Really."

Darla's pain and Randy's terror. Watching him tell the story, it was still hard for me to see him as a murderer.

"So why didn't you call for help when you realized she was dead?"

"I didn't know she was dead. I hoped she was just unconscious, and if I left her there, she'd be gone in the morning." He consciously clasped his hands and placed them in his lap, trying to stay in control.

"And when nobody had checked Aaron's office by noon, you went in and discovered the body."

Randy took his glasses off and rubbed his eyes.

"I wanted her to be all right. I hoped—I prayed—that she had gotten up and left sometime during the night. But she was lying there. And there was nothing I could do for her. The only thing I could do then was protect the university. That was why I asked Curtis to get rid of the camera. I hid the tiger because I had a fantasy that the police would think she had been murdered by a transient who had taken the tiger with him. Then no one on campus would be blamed." He put his glasses back on, but he still didn't look at me.

"I understand why you took the tiger. But why did you decide to visit Helen Stern?" I had a little trouble getting that one out.

"The only way I could think of to remove suspicion from Aaron without attracting it to myself was to direct it at someone else—which was why Roger Wade hired you, after all, to find another suspect." He glanced up at me, then back down at his hands, which were threatening to escape control once more. "I had planned to simply leave the tiger in the therapist's office and then suggest to you that a search might be a good idea. That way I would be out of it."

"You didn't need to carry a gun just to plant the tiger, did you?"

"I was frightened. I was beginning to feel like a criminal, and I felt a need to protect myself." There was something self-righteous about the way he said that, as if feeling like a criminal wasn't somehow connected to having committed a crime.

"When did you decide to stage a fake suicide?"

"I'm not sure. The front door of the therapist's house was unlocked, so I walked in. She discovered me standing outside her office, and when I told her who I was, she suggested that we talk. She thought Aaron was the murderer—she actually thought I might help convict him—and I'm not certain what I said that led her to believe I might be involved." Randy suddenly bolted from the chair, the way cats spring straight upward from a sitting position.

He stopped himself before he reached the door.

"She told me I had to go to the police." He turned back to face me as he said it. "I replied that I couldn't, and I pulled out the gun to show her I was serious. She picked up the phone to call them herself. She was so harsh, so determined that I had to be punished. I couldn't handle that. So I reached across the desk and shot her."

"What about the open drawer?"

"I wanted to know what was in Darla Hayden's file. I was going to remove anything that would point to anyone at the university. I had the most recent piece of paper in my hands, the one with the girl's new address, when you came in." He took a deep breath and blurted, "I just wanted to scare you when I shot through the door. I knew the shot was high."

"Thanks." I remembered how terrified I had felt, hiding behind the tree. I lost a little of my sympathy for him. I remembered finding Helen Stern's body. The remaining few drops drained out through my toes.

"What do we do now?" he asked.

"We tell the story to the police," I said. "The station isn't far. If you don't want me to call them, we can walk over there."

"But you were willing to help Aaron. Why aren't you willing to help me? I can afford to hire you. The money wouldn't be a problem." The long-fingered hands fluttered over his sparse hair again.

"The short answer to that has to do with presumption of innocence versus confession of guilt." There was a longer answer, but I'd have to think about it.

"I'm not going to the police. Don't you understand that yet?" The hands dropped to his sides. He pulled a gun out of his pocket and pointed it at me.

I should have been expecting that, I know. Even puppies sometimes bite. I still froze in my seat.

"Put the gun down, Randy. Please don't point the gun at me. You can't cover up any longer." I watched the gun barrel waver. I lifted a hand slowly, easing my desk drawer open, not moving any unnecessary muscles. "It may not be that bad. Roger Wade will defend you. The jury may find you sympathetic."

"The jury? The jury? My God! Who knows what a jury will think? The jury might find that disturbed student sympathetic!" His hands went out of control again, carrying the gun toward the ceiling.

I pulled the one I had taken from Aaron Hiller out of my desk drawer and pointed it at his chest.

"That's enough," I said. "Put the gun down slowly, all the way to the floor."

"Or what? Or what?" Froth appeared at the corner of Randy Thurman's mouth. "Or you'll shoot me? Is that it? You'll shoot me?"

My heart lurched at the thought but my hand didn't quiver. I stared him straight in the eye. If somebody had to be a victim, he could have the honor.

"Yes. I'll shoot."

He giggled, a burbly sound as if he were a drowning man expelling the last air from his lungs.

"Don't bother," he said.

Before I could move, Thurman brought the gun to his temple and fired. I sat in my chair and watched him fall.

# Chapter
## 15

THE BLACK-AND-WHITE ARRIVED within moments after I called. I waited for the officers on the porch and explained I would have to talk with them there. In fact, I didn't go back in my office until after everyone, including Matthews and the medical examiner, was long gone.

By then it was too late to catch Roger Wade before his appearance on the six o'clock news. Nevertheless, he agreed to change his statement in time for the news at eleven. I was sort of hoping he'd have the grace to apologize, but I wasn't really surprised when he didn't.

I pulled out the spare blanket that Ramona had used and spread it over my blood-stained carpet. The red spatters on the wall were already turning brown. There was nothing I could do to hide them—they were too dispersed.

I knew that Curtis would want me to call him, but I was afraid the news of Randy's suicide would upset him so much that I'd have to comfort him, and I couldn't do that just yet.

Instead, I called Deke. He arrived fifteen minutes later

with a bucket of chicken. After glancing at the speckled wall and the blanket on the carpet, he unplugged the phone and moved me from the office to the living room.

"There had to be something I could have done differently," I said as he handed me a drumstick and a napkin.

"Why you?" he asked. "You didn't shoot anybody."

"No. But I was somehow involved in a step-by-step progression that ended with Randy Thurman shooting himself."

Butch hopped up on the coffee table. Deke grabbed the bucket. I tore a hunk of flesh off the drumstick and coaxed the cat down. I tore a second hunk and gave it to Sundance, who had been waiting beside my ankle.

"I don't suppose you'd be willing to shut them in the other room," Deke said.

"Sorry. But large pieces keep them busy and fill them up fairly rapidly." I took a small bite for myself.

"Aaron Hiller did some bad shit. Randy Thurman made some mistakes and then did some bad shit on top of that. I don't see where you did anything but your job. You did what you were paid to do, and then did your best for the Rodriguezes because it was right. Do you have any beer?"

"In the refrigerator." I stripped a breast for the cats while I waited for him to get two bottles. I wiped my hands on the napkin before accepting one. "Doing my job. I'm back to feeling I shouldn't have accepted this one."

"Because you don't like the way it turned out. But that don't do you no good. You couldn't have known at the beginning that you wouldn't like the end. And if you hadn't been there, maybe Thurman would have managed to fake the shrink's suicide."

The thought cheered me, if only a little.

"Can they get Aaron Hiller for any of this?" Deke asked.

"I don't know. Probably not. With Thurman dead, he can argue that he didn't lay a hand on Darla—only another part of his anatomy—and nobody can contradict him. I hope he was right when he said he was ruined no matter how this ended. I really do hope that. I hope his wife leaves him, too." I tore up another breast for the cats, ignoring Deke's disapproval. They slowed down a little as they chewed. I picked up a second drumstick for myself.

"Hiller's wife won't leave him, and that anchorwoman won't lose her job. Those are the only two things you can count on. Except yourself. You can count on yourself, and that means you can get over this." Deke found the one breast I hadn't given to the cats and started in on it.

"I have to talk to Rick and Gabriela," I said. "They said Darla Hayden was the worst case, but there were others. Maybe I can work this out by helping them make the case for the class-action suit."

"Against the university? You want to do that?"

"I have to think about it. I might. I have to think about it," I repeated.

"You do what you have to do," he said.

The long-term fallout of any case is impossible to predict. In the short term, I offered my services to Rick and Gabriela Rodriguez, pro bono, to investigate sexual harassment and criminal exploitation of graduate students on campus, provided they could produce at least one student with evidence that would stand up in court. I'm still waiting. Which only means that the proper combination of a student with evidence and the willingness to persevere through a jury trial hasn't arisen.

Although Aaron Hiller wasn't charged with a crime in connection with Darla Hayden—and Jeannie didn't leave him, to my disappointment—he hasn't been on *Nightline* again. He hasn't even been on the Channel 12 News at Eleven.

But he did make the newspaper. Sandra and I found two of his former amours who agreed to admit publicly that he had beaten them up. She included that—and a detailed description of the injuries inflicted—in her long retrospective on the Darla Hayden case. Someone sprayed the word KILLER on Aaron's Lexus, and he has kept a lower profile ever since. The university worked out a deal where he keeps his affiliation, but he doesn't have to actually teach classes.

The check I got from working on the case more than paid for new carpet and new paint in my office. Blood money. Ramona insisted on picking out and paying for new client chairs. They had padded backs and seats, covered in black-and-white cowhide. They even had shiny black arms. She wanted to buy me the matching desk chair, too. I refused, but I broke down and bought it for myself after I saw the new ones actually in my office.

Brianne McKinley moved to a network-owned and operated station in Los Angeles, bringing Curtis's consulting job to a neat conclusion. Sandra, who still follows those things, said Brianne took the station from third place to first in the ratings.

Sandra even forgave me for breaking the dinner date when I told her the whole story.

This time, Curtis was tougher. He was truly angry that I not only hadn't called him to let him know what had happened, I hadn't even answered the phone when he had tried to get me. I didn't blame him. In his place, I wouldn't have understood. We finally settled on a dinner date to talk it out.

I showed up at his apartment with a bag of takeout Chinese, including scallops with yellow chives, and a companion bag of videotapes, including *The Third Man*, a noncolorized *Casablanca*, and the original *Stagecoach*. He picked *Stagecoach*.

It was a good choice. You don't think John Wayne and Claire Trevor can possibly get together. But they do.